True
Rainbow

T0054191

True
Rainbow

CHERRY TSAI JOYAL

TATE PUBLISHING
AND **ENTERPRISES,** LLC

Published by Tate Publishing & Enterprises, LLC
127 E. Trade Center Terrace | Mustang, Oklahoma 73064 USA
1.888.361.9473 | www.tatepublishing.com

Tate Publishing is committed to excellence in the publishing industry. The company reflects the philosophy established by the founders, based on Psalm 68:11,
"The Lord gave the word and great was the company of those who published it."

Book design copyright © 2014 by Tate Publishing, LLC. All rights reserved.
Cover design by Rtor Maghuyop
Interior design by Honeylette Pino

Published in the United States of America

ISBN: 978-1-62994-619-1
1. Fiction / General
2. Fiction / Religious
14.01.14

In loving memory of my father…

ACKNOWLEDGMENTS

I want to humbly thank God for bestowing upon me this story. I pray that whoever reads this book will be inspired by God's unfailing love, and be richly blessed.

I want to thank my husband Bob for his non-stop loving support and encouragement. Also, my gratitude goes to my family and Bob's family for their trust and love.

Special thanks to all my friends who walk alongside me in this spiritual journey.

Contents

CHAPTER 1

Unfortunately, I was there in my dorm room when Poppa phoned to complain in his deaf man's shout. "We teach you to be a lady so you can marry a good boy in town so we don't need to worry about you. Look at your two younger sisters; they're both married without college degrees. Your Mama married me when she turned seventeen. Why bother your brain with unnecessary junk? Life is cruel to women especially. If you don't do anything about getting married soon, you will turn into an old maid before you know it." He sighed so loud that I knew it would make me miserable for the rest of the week.

Poppa was a farmer and Mama a housewife. My two older brothers and two younger sisters still lived in my hometown, Athens, Alabama. I, the black sheep, had left home at eighteen, to pursue a college degree. From 6 a.m. to noon I worked at the library on campus, and from 6 p.m. to 10 p.m. I waited tables at a restaurant. It was not easy living far from home and I did miss my family and country living. I missed the scent of grass and wild flowers that popped out of nowhere after the first rain in the spring, the smell of fresh raw milk, newly hatched eggs, whole-grain bread with home made butter, not to mention the aroma of honey baked ham and bacon from the old style cooking. On the one hand, the laidback country atmosphere permeated so deep into my skin that it mesmerized me to no end, but on the other hand it bored me to death so much that I wanted to yawn all day.

Growing up as the oldest girl in the family, I had to help out with all the chores. From cooking to cleaning, Mama made sure I did not miss any wrinkles ironing the clothes, or any mandated seasoning in the cooking, but when I reached age fifteen, I knew I had to get out. Life had so much to offer outside the farm. I didn't want to grow old doing laundry and dishes, or chasing chickens all day.

So I came to Los Angeles, to chase my dreams. One good thing about LA was that people there were too busy to notice me so I was left alone daydreaming about my future. I loved art, but was not gifted enough to draw a straight line; I loved dancing, but was not coordinated enough to stand on one toe; and I loved poems, but was not talented enough to make sentences rhyme. Sometimes I wondered whether my dreams were just bubbles. *Will I be left with no choice one day but to pack up my ripped jeans and go home?*

One Wednesday morning in March, I was working at the library putting books back on the shelves. Around six o'clock, I heard a knock on the door. The library didn't open until 7:30, so I ignored the knock. That person kept knocking, however, so I went to the door and yelled, "Stop knocking! The library stays dark until 7:30."

"Oh, No." he said calmly. "I need these articles right away so I can finish my research before I present it to the dean's office. Besides, your library is anything but dark; you have all the lights on." Then he showed his teeth, in a boyish smile.

I must have chuckled. The man standing in front of me had a mustache, and long reddish hair in a ponytail. He was skinny and tall, probably no more than forty years old. He looked Irish to me, with his fair skin, and lazy but warm eyes behind thick lenses. I did not find him attractive but there was something about him that made me very comfortable.

"Sir, I am sorry. I have rules to obey, and you just have to wait." I said. I was only a clerk, and on top of that, I was a student. Students were taught to obey rules.

He paced back and forth in front of me, and kept tapping his watch. I felt so bad that I said, "Sir, if this is indeed urgent, you can give me the titles of the books or articles, and I will try to find them for you."

His face lit up. "Really? You would do that for me? That's very kind of you."

I felt this big halo above my head, so I obtained the list from him, rushed in, gathered all but one book, and rushed out.

"Sir, *Capitalism and Freedom* was checked out to Professor Thompson a month ago. He hasn't returned it. It probably is sitting on his bookshelf somewhere. Do you happen to know him? I have heard from other students that he is tough and mean." I handed him a pile of books and articles.

Looking down, he kept nodding his head, "Oh, I see. It just so happens that I am he." Then he looked straight at me. His eyes no longer looked droopy but animated.

"You are Professor Thom-? Oh. I am so sorry." I was so embarrassed that I wanted to dig a hole and jump in.

"Don't worry about it. You are not the first person to call me names, and, trust me, you won't be the last. Does that make you feel better?" He started walking away, still carrying on the conversation. "But I want to thank you for all your effort in finding these articles. I will tell the Dean that *Capitalism and Freedom* is missing because it was checked out to a tough and mean professor whom we won't name, so you will be off the hook."

He turned and gave me another smile. "I like your southern accent. Very pleasant to the ears."

I felt light headed. I liked his compliment. No one had ever said that before. Besides, Professor Thompson was a well-known and respected professor in Political Science.

I must have stood at the same spot admiring his back for a long while. *What a gentleman Professor Thompson is! And he is charming too!*

After that encounter, Professor Thompson showed up at the library pretty often. My heart would pound hard and my breathing would turn heavy as he walked by me. He came by several times asking for my help in locating several research papers. I knew he was pretty capable of finding them himself, but of course I did not mind lending my help.

Two weeks passed, and we still stayed at the same routine of "Hi," "thank you," "you are welcome," "bye." Then one day before he bid good-bye, he asked me, "Are you by any chance free tonight?" He blinked behind the lenses, and I was tempted to nod my head off, but then I realized I had to work at the restaurant.

"I would love to, but I have to work tonight. I am sorry."

"What time do you get off work?"

"A quarter after ten. Why?"

He smiled, "Maybe I can buy you a late night snack afterwards, if you are up for it."

My face must have glowed. "Where?" I asked. Every single trick my sisters taught me such as playing hard to get or pretending I didn't care flew out of the window.

"I can stop by your restaurant around ten and we can decide from there. Sound good?" He looked at me with a twinkle in his eyes.

I nodded. I gave him the name and address of the restaurant where I worked on Santa Monica Blvd. He left. I looked at his back as he walked away. Then he turned and smiled at me. I waved back.

For the rest of the day, I was exceedingly cheerful. Quite a few coworkers gave me a weird look. One even asked, "What on earth is going on with you? Did you win the lottery or what?"

Lottery? Who cares about a lottery? I am in love!

CHAPTER 2

We had a great late night snack at one of the coffee shops near Santa Monica Pier. Professor Thompson was a gentleman; he biked me home after our date. When I held on behind him, feeling the breeze, my heart started singing an unknown romantic melody.

Brian was nothing but wonderful, intelligent, and smart. I was hesitant to tell him my simple life story, but he seemed totally amazed by my hometown and my family. He had had a very complicated life. His parents divorced when he was eight. His mom gave up custody so he stayed with his dad, who was an ambassador at the time, and traveled with him all over the world.

"Before I could rest my feet and call a place home, we were ready to pack up and leave again," Brian said, as his eyes met mine. "After I'd traveled so much, I was longing for stability, yearning for home.

"My father packed my schedule with four tutors who taught me foreign languages, literature, history, politics, science, math, piano, and violin."

"Wow! Your life was full of excitement. I wish mine had been like that."

His face became downcast as he replied. "The childhood I remember was books after books, classes after classes, and maids after maids. Then I missed my mother so much that I took a trip to France to see her, when I was old enough, for I was told she had moved to Paris. I stood before her front window for two hours, and then I left and went home."

"Why?"

He did not answer me right away. He sipped the coffee, "I saw her through the windows. She was holding a little girl, and a little boy was leaning against her. Then there was this man sitting by her playing piano. They were singing and talking. She looked content and happy with her new family."

"You left because you were happy for your mother? It doesn't make sense."

"No, I left because I felt abandoned. How could she be so happy with other kids but not me? I missed her so much but she did not seem to miss me at all." He looked down to stir his coffee.

"How do you know she did not miss you?" I knew his feelings must have been hurt.

"My father told me she remarried not long after she had left us, but that is not the point. Had she missed me, she would have come back to look for me, or written letters to me, right? Besides, she looked so happy that I felt jealous. Why couldn't she be happy with my father and me? Why did she have to leave us when I needed her the most?" The crease between his eyebrows deepened.

"That's not true. You don't define happiness by the way it looks on the surface. Let's say if you polled one hundred people who appeared to be happy, you asked them the question whether they are truly happy, you'd be surprised by the majority of answers. For example, I asked my two sisters who are married with kids whether they were happy? You know what their response was? They looked at me as if I were from another planet.

Happy? Happy for what? Are you crazy? We have no time for that. That's their answer.

"You did not ask your mom in person. She probably missed you a lot, and there was a big void in her heart which you would never be able to detect from the outside."

He looked at me in disbelief. "You are very honest and straightforward. On top of that, you have this pair of curious eyes that are so encouraging that people are obliged to pour their hearts out to you. It is as if I had no choice but to spill out my true feelings. I used to not trust women because of my past experiences, but you are different. On the one hand you are simple, while on the other you are thoughtful and caring. Vivian, you make people around you feel very special and comfortable."

"Am I? No one ever complimented me like that. My family thinks that I daydream too much and ask too many questions."

I realized it was almost midnight. The staff was waiting for us to leave so they could close shop. They were too nice to suggest it, but I could feel the impatience in their stares.

As we walked out, he posed the question. "So are you happy?"

"Oh, yeah! Especially right now!" I laughed. "How about you? Are you happy?"

"I wish I could grab the happiness I am experiencing this moment, place it in my pocket, and take it out whenever I feel blue."

"Professor Thompson, if you are successful in finding the formula for true happiness, please mass produce it so others will benefit from it. In fact, better yet, you should package the happiness in a bottle, patent it, and then sell it."

"It sounds great! And I will share the patent and profits with you."

"Really? You will share the patent and profits with me?" I was deeply touched. No one had ever promised such a silly thing to me. He knew my love language.

Along the way to my dorm, we were talking, joking and laughing. I had not had such a heartfelt laugh for a long time.

We clicked! We could talk about anything and everything. For the next few days, we biked through the city of Santa Monica, from one end to the other, splashing joy and laughs at every corner. My friends called us lovebirds because we were inseparable. We held hands everywhere we went. Many times stares came our way but Brian shrugged them off.

"Life is too short to worry about other people's views, especially if they are bystanders'." Brian said.

He would wait for me outside my classroom or I would sneak into his classes to sit in the back and listen to his lecture. As soon as he spotted me, his eyes sparkled and his face radiated. Then he would use every opportunity to walk by me to give me a gentle touch.

"I feel like eighteen again," He said. "I wish I can announce to the whole world I am in love."

I laughed. "Yes, you can!"

So we ran to a remote site of the campus and he shouted at the top of his lungs, "I love Vivian and she loves me."

We spun as fast as we could and laughed until we were out of breath. Then we tumbled onto the grass, listening to each other's heartbeats. Brian took my hand, kissed it, and placed it over his heart.

"My heart belongs to you, Vivian Lewis. May you keep it and treasure it."

CHAPTER 3

Six months later, Brian knelt down and proposed to me. I accepted his hand. I was on the top of the world and could not wait to share this big news with my family. I called home that same evening. "Mama, I am getting married!"

My mother was very excited for me, but then she turned over the phone to the head of the household—Poppa.

"Who is he? Do we know him?"

I explained to him that Brian was a well-respected professor with a wonderful job and a good salary. I told him Brian was a good person, with integrity, and above all he liked my southern accent.

"How old is he, if he is a professor?"

"He is forty-five." I did not expect age would become an issue.

Poppa almost screamed. "He is one foot in the grave already. Vivian, you are only twenty-one. Your life just started but he is already in his sunset years."

What does sunset years mean? Brian does not have one foot in the grave. His two feet are standing on solid ground. That was what I wanted to tell Poppa, but I knew he would have blown up.

"Poppa! I am going to be twenty-two in a few months. Besides, he has great health and he looks much younger than his age—"

"No matter how many times I shined my thirty-year old trailer trying to keep it new, it is still a thirty-year old piece of junk. Years don't lie. Don't be fooled by his appearance. Vivian, do you know how old your Poppa is?"

"I know Poppa is young."

"I am fifty. Big Five-O. Can you imagine your Poppa is only fifty and is going to have a son-in-law the same age? Let's forget about he's asking for your hand. If he is so desperate to become a part of the family, why don't I just adopt him as my brother, and you can call him uncle.

"Vivian, he is much older with a lot of experiences, but you are green and gullible, so of course you fell for him. It won't be a good match. He is too old for you. If you really want to get married, come home and we will find you a good young boy. Your two brothers and I were just talking about you the other day, and they were eager to find you a perfect husband.

"Your old professor probably was divorced, which is a big no no. Why do you want to buy a used car if you can get a brand new one in better condition at a cheaper price?"

"Poppa, he has never been married before."

"He is forty-five and has never been married?" Poppa got more suspicious, "That's even worse. He must have had some serious plumbing problems. Vivian, listen to me. You are confused right now. You are not thinking straight.

"I saw this young boy on the farm working hard, sweating, so I invited him to the house and gave him a glass of iced tea. He saw your picture in the living room and asked about you. Vivian, there are many young boys here waiting for you to throw your handkerchief, or just a glance."

"Poppa, I don't love other boys that way. Brian is the only one I've ever felt connected to. We clicked. Poppa, just as you were connected to Mama—"

"What clicked? What connection? Your Mama and I had a marriage arranged by your grandparents, and our marriage turned out just fine. You young people are so brainwashed by the TV and movies that you have to find some kind of soul mates through soul searching, not to mention the divorce rate is at its peak now. Most of the time you don't even know what life or marriage is all about.

"Vivian, do you know you are going to be a widow if he dies? How many years do you think you can be celebrating together? Are you facing reality, or are you out of your mind? That's why I warned your mother that the college degree would do more harm than good to your common sense. You see, this is exactly what I had predicted. I am always right!" Poppa's breathing was getting heavier.

"Poppa, this is my life and my reality, even if he has to die early. Please let me face my life on my own terms, so I can embrace it without fear or regret. I have lived too long with fear, and I don't want to do that any more." I was fighting back my tears as I yelled at him.

Poppa seemed to stop breathing. I yelled, "Poppa! Poppa!"

After two minutes, his voice returned. It was as chilling as frost. "If it is your choice that your Mama and I have no say in this matter, go ahead and plan your wedding without us either. We want no part in it." He hung up.

I couldn't believe my ears. I dropped flat on my bed and my mind started racing. I bit my lip till it bled. *How could this be happening? My parents just disowned me. They did not want to have anything to do with my wedding or me. A wedding without their blessing meant nothing. I would walk down the aisle as the world's loneliest bride.*

When I met up with Brian that night at our favorite coffee shop, I could not stop my tears from falling. He pondered and said, "Vivian, your father is right. I might not be there for you in ten or twenty years. Do you want to reconsider my proposal?"

I couldn't believe my ears. After all the battles I had gone through protecting him from my own father, Brian turned around to side with him. *What about my feelings?*

"What are you talking about? You don't want to marry me?"

Brian took hold of my hands and looked into my eyes, "Vivian, I love you more than anything. I have never been more serious in my life than when I asked you to marry me. You are the first woman I can trust with my whole heart."

"So what do you mean?"

"Let me ask you this question: What if I died a couple of years from now? Who is going to take care of you? Will you still love me if you have to push the wheelchair around or bathe me in bed?" Brian looked very serious.

I thought for a moment. "Brian, first off, life does not guarantee longevity. Let me ask you the same questions: Will you take care of me if these things happen to me instead?"

"Of course."

"So why do you think otherwise when it comes to me? You think love is a one-way street? Or do you think I am so shallow when it comes to love that I can only deal with good times but not hardship? I might be twenty-three years younger than you are but it doesn't mean my love is worth less. If you want to withdraw your proposal, please feel free to say it. Don't just drag me into your pathetic reasoning for backing out or make me a scapegoat to cover your cowardice."

Brian was stunned. Still holding my hands, he said, "Vivian, I am sorry to make you feel that way. I am not a coward and have never backed down from my stance in my whole life if I knew I was in the right. You know I am all by myself after my father had passed. However this is your family that you care so much about and I don't want you to lose yours because of me. Is there anything I can do to change your family's views?"

I looked at him. I was touched by his sincerity. He cared about my family because he cared about me.

"We can go visit them, so they can get to know you better." I said, with this big question mark in the back of my mind. I knew it was a do-or-die call.

He nodded. "Let's do it! They have the first right of refusal, right?"

"Are you sure it is not called Veto Right?"

He hugged me, and sighed. I closed my eyes wishing for a calm and peaceful meeting between him and my family, at least not anything that would lead to World War III.

CHAPTER 4

We planned a trip home during the Spring break. I had never seen Brian so nervous. He was constantly checking his shirt and tie to make sure they were properly aligned. He kept asking me if he looked presentable. I felt like teasing him but realized it would be too cruel.

"What are your parents, brothers, and sisters like?" He asked.

"Oh, they are all like your next door neighbors, but several things to bear in mind: Poppa doesn't hear well. You have to speak loud to his left ear, if he allows you to approach him, of course. Always keep arms-length distance from him because he doesn't like people to get too close. Mama is the sweetest lady in the whole wide world. Her life revolves about her husband and her kids. Her mission in life is to make sure no one goes to bed hungry, and none of her children get harmed. Josh is your straightforward kind of guy with a soft heart, but he can get stubborn at times. Never try to get on his bad side. Since he was the first-born son, he carries more weight than anyone of us and he believes in the Second Amendment rights." I peeked to see Brian's response, knowing his anti-gun feelings.

Brian didn't blink. He looked serious as he said. "I have no ill feelings toward my fellow citizens who support the right to bear arms, as long as they don't point their guns at me."

I suppressed my laugh and continued, "Paul is the second son of the family. He is shy and soft spoken. You would never guess that he has won many trophies in debating. He is a teacher at a local school."

"He seems like my kind of guy."

"Victoria, about a year younger than me, is a busy-body. By the way, she loves gifts, the more expensive the better. She has this high-pitched voice that can penetrate your brain. Oh, she takes pleasure in getting on people's nerves. Elizabeth is the youngest but she is also the smartest. Never try to fool her."

"I thought you were the smartest one in the family?"

"No, I am the prettiest! You forgot."

"You are the smartest one plus the prettiest one, all in one package! I got the best deal!" Brian hugged me and then tickled me.

When we landed at the airport, my oldest brother, Josh, came to pick us up. He looked Brian up and down, but avoided direct eye contact. When Brian offered a handshake, Josh simply ignored it. He grabbed our luggage, rushed us to his truck, and then sped off. Brian and I tried to make chitchat with Josh, but his lips were so airtight that pretty soon we realized we were making fools of ourselves. We gave up.

Brian switched his attention to the scenery. He turned to me several times and exclaimed, "Vivian, I have never been so close to nature in my whole life. Do you see cows, horses, and sheep out there? Wouldn't this be a great painting? I can picture you running around barefoot in the pasture with wild flowers and blue sky in the backdrop. The only color I remember from my childhood was gray—gray buildings, gray walls, gray doors, and gray sky. The rest of the colors didn't seem to exist."

Hidden inside this middle-aged man was a little boy longing to jump out to spy on the world. He was mesmerized by the spectrum of colors the nature offered.

The ice wrapped around Josh started to melt. He realized Brian was genuine. Josh pointed at a farm on the left hand side and said, "Hey, guys, that is my ranch. We just bought twenty calves. If you are interested, I can show you how to be a real cowboy." He looked at Brian through the rear view mirror.

Brian was excited. "You mean you will show me how to milk the cow?"

"Anything. You name it! If you find it in the book, I will show you in real life. No nonsense." Josh was really proud of himself when it came to his territory.

"Deal!" That was the loudest word I had ever heard from Brian.

They made a pact.

I did not want to say anything to spoil the moment. Josh's opinion carried a lot of weight around Poppa.

"Hey, Josh, how old is Green Pea now?" I asked him about his oldest son Peter.

"Oh, he is getting *so* big. Within a year or two, he is gonna be taller than you are, Sis. Can you believe how time flies! He is gonna be eight in two months. Sis, he still remembers the little soldiers you gave him for his sixth year birthday. He loves bugs and snakes but hates math, prefers guns to pens, just like his old man."

Josh was laughing. It went without saying—he was a proud dad.

Once Josh's shield was off, we were able to talk about everything under the sun. He had a southern hospitality and charm in him that no one could resist, which was how he had earned his beautiful bride's heart ten years ago.

"How many kids do you have?" Brian asked.

"Well! I am not as productive as Poppa, but I am trying my best to catch up. I have three kiddos now, and the fourth one is coming."

Brian turned to me, "I want at least four, too." Then he winked at me.

Josh looked at us from the rearview mirror, "It is hard to raise kids these days, and they don't appreciate you. They think that money grows on trees and that they deserve every drop of my sweat. I used to dream that when they grew up they would help me run my ranch so I could retire early, but I don't think that anymore. Trust me, this kids-rearing business is way harder than raising cows and horses. For the herds and flocks, as long as you throw them straw they are fine and dandy, at least they don't snap at you, but when it comes to kids, I tell ya—" Josh pretended to sigh.

Brian posed a question out of the blue. "But you will never give up any of your children, right? No matter what kind of circumstances you are in."

I knew right away where it was heading. He was connecting the dots to his mother.

"No way. They are my kids, from the day they were born till the day I die. No matter how ugly or stinky they are, they are mine all right. No one dares to touch them."

I touched Josh's shoulder, "Hey, Josh, do you happen to know what is for dinner tonight? Mama is such a good cook. Brian, you have to try my mom's cooking, she is well known for her beef stew and pea soup, right, Josh?"

Josh recited tonight's dinner menu: Baked potato, beef stew, fresh baked corn bread, roasted chicken, beef, honey baked ham, pea soup, etc.

He noticed Brian's quietness, "What happened to him? Doesn't he like any of those dishes? It is too late to ask Mama to change the menu."

Brian placed his hand on Josh's back, "I love them all. No worries." Then Brian looked at me and smiled. I could tell he wanted to fit in to my family and be accepted.

We got to the house. It was as packed as usual, and I knew it was a shock to Brian, for he was seldom surrounded by lots of loud and curious strangers. I smiled at him before I was pushed into the kitchen. Mama stood in front of the oven checking if the chicken's skin had turned golden color. As she painted another layer of butter and seasoning on it, she saw me and grabbed me, "What kind of meat does he like?"

Before I could answer, Victoria said, "Vivian, he looks too serious. He frowns too much. Does he ever smile? The good part about him is that he still has a full head of hair, unlike Poppa, even though I am not fond of his red hair."

Elizabeth, my youngest sister, said, "He looks handsome, though. No wonder you like him."

"You should not judge a book by its cover." Mama sounded like an old sage.

"Mama, you should know me better than that." I felt insulted.

Someone nudged me from the back. It was Grace, my sister-in-law, Josh's wife. I gave her a big hug and noticed her belly was really big. "Oh my goodness. I knew you were pregnant, but did not know the baby is ready to pop out. How many months now?"

Grace rubbed her stomach and smiled, "Almost seven months now. I think it's a boy. He kicks a lot. I hope he is not as naughty as his brothers though."

"It might be a good thing if he were a boy. But if it turns out to be a girl and looks like Josh; oh, she will be in big trouble." Victoria always liked to spoil the moment.

I pushed her away and placed my hand on Grace, "don't listen to her. What she meant was, if the baby is a girl, she will look like you."

Then I realized I haven't seen Ruth, the other sister-in-law. "Where is Ruth?"

Suddenly the air froze. No one talked or moved.

Mama broke the silence, "Ruth left."

"Ruth left, just like that? What happened? When did she leave? When is she coming back? What about Paul? Where is he?" I was at a complete loss.

Elizabeth held my hand, "Vivian, I'll tell you later. But please remember at the dinner table, *Do not* mention anything about Ruth, not to Poppa or to Paul."

"What about the kids? Meagan and Jay, are they all right?"

"They stay with me for now. They are fine. You will see them, but don't ask anything, all right?" Elizabeth was encumbered with concerns.

Mama sighed softly but said nothing. Grace gave me a signal to drop the subject.

As soon as the dinner bell rang, everyone rushed over to the table. Right after Poppa said the grace, all the kids extended their arms and forks fighting for chicken thighs and breasts, roast beef, and the garlic bread.

Poppa suddenly yelled, "Stop! Where are your table manners? We have guests here!" Suddenly all the hands stopped in mid-air. I looked at Poppa with a question mark: *since when did I become a guest?*

Tears streamed down from Meagan's eyes.

Brian looked at her and then looked at me. "I wish I had brothers or sisters to fight over the food at the dinner table."

However, he was rubbing Poppa the wrong way, so Poppa instantly said, "We are talking about manners here. Kids need rules to follow. As long as they are under my roof, they have to obey the rules." He was staring at Brian, awaiting further challenges. His hair stood on end. He was like a pit bull ready to fight.

"Mr. Lewis, I can see how good discipline has reflected on Vivian as well as everyone in your household. That's why I respect and love her so much. I did not mean to challenge your authority, and if I made you feel that way, I apologize. It was never my intention."

Mama said, "Let's eat. Brian, I heard you liked beef stew. Try it and see whether it suits your taste. Hey, Poppa, if you don't start using your fork and knife, no one will dare to touch the food. The duty of the head of household is to make your guests feel at home." As usual, Mama came to the rescue. I felt like jumping over to give her a big hug.

Poppa shut up. He threw Brian a quick glance. Realizing, number one, that Brian was not on the offense, and number two, that the dinner table was a cease-fire zone. He quietly picked up the salad bowl, threw some green salad on his plate, and then passed the bowl to Josh. Suddenly the room and the dinner table came back alive.

I relaxed a bit, and squeezed Brian's hand, signaling that the situation was not that bad. He turned to give me a wry smile alluding the war was far from over.

In my family, we had a tradition of casting votes for decision-making, especially when it came to big decisions. Poppa called it "democracy", but he reserved his veto right. When it was necessary he would exercise his special authority, but so far he had only used it twice.

I knew my low approval rating in the house, and I needed at least fifty percent of the votes in order for Brian to be accepted, provided that Poppa did not exercise his veto right. So as the dinner went on, I was pondering whose votes I had won thus far. I knew Mama, Elizabeth, her husband, Bruce, and Grace were on my side, while Poppa, Victoria, her husband, Leo, and Josh might object. So I had four "Yes" votes against four "No" votes, which left Paul in the middle.

I desperately needed his vote on this matter since Ruth was not there rooting for me.

What has happened to Ruth, though? She is such a sweet girl. I hope nothing bad has happened to her.

Poppa exchanged several comments with Brian. Several times Mama had to cut in to ease the tension. Josh was also into politics, which was Brian's strongest interest, but they did not see eye-to-eye on every current event so they would engage in some heated debates. Paul quietly ate his food the whole time. He seemed lost without Ruth. My heart sank deep. Paul was always the cheerful one in the family, but his eyes no longer sparkled and his face no longer glowed.

Elizabeth and Bruce constantly checked on the kids to make sure they were upbeat, not bored to death by the adult conversations. Victoria chatted with Leo about their convenience store and what items they needed to replenish for the coming season. I glanced over the dinner table and felt a sense of belonging that I thought I had long lost. For my whole life I had tried to run away from this noisy and boring house, and yet it still held my deepest yearning. *Is this a sort of awakening?*

Then I realized it was Brian who had made me realize my family was a blessing instead of a burden. No matter how crazy it drove me or how unbearable it seemed at times, it was still a big part of me.

After dinner, Poppa ordered me to show Brian the house and the back porch. I knew he was about to collect votes from all parties. Before I left the room, I quickly swung around the circle of Mama, Josh, and

Paul, begging them with teary puppy eyes. Mama assured me she was on my side, but I had no idea where Paul and Josh stood.

After this meeting, my parents and family accepted Brian and embraced our marriage. I gave thanks to Paul's additional vote on top of others', so I thought.

Not long after, Brian and I had a simple wedding at a local church with my immediate family and our close friends. It was the church where Poppa and Mama had attended every Sunday for their whole lives, and where I was forced to attend on many Sundays when I was little. Pastor Daniel, who ministered my wedding, was not only Poppa's Best Man at his wedding, but also the pastor who married all of my siblings.

Poppa walked me down the aisle and reluctantly handed me over to Brian. After he answered the priest, he whispered into Brian's ear that he'd better take good care of me, or else he would never be able to sleep at night. Brian patted his back and assured him with all his heart. Everyone except Ruth came to our wedding. That was the most beautiful and memorable day of our lives.

Then I found out on that faithful night of casting votes, Paul played a much bigger role than giving us his pivotal vote.

He convinced everyone to accept Brian to the family.

CHAPTER 5

I thought marrying to Brian would guarantee a life happily ever after. Being called "Mrs. Thompson" did tickle my ears for a few weeks, until I realized Professor Thompson did nothing at home but reading, researching, and writing. At first I tried to bribe him to do something like fixing toilets or plumbing but pretty soon I discovered he did not have those skills.

I knew more about tools than he did, and he would just sit reading the instructions and criticize the manual's bad grammar or typos. I was so amused that I would just pick up tools, and start to fix whatever was broken.

"Wow! How did you do that? How did you figure that out? The manual didn't tell you to screw it or connect those two pieces together. You are pretty handy." Brian would give me a round of applause.

"It is called common sense, my dear!" I sometimes felt flattered. Then Brian would give me this naughty smile. I still have no idea whether he really did not have common sense or he simply didn't want to get his hands dirty. Except that, Brian was a wonderful husband.

Eighteen months after we got married, I had Michael. During my pregnancy I had no morning sickness so I didn't even know I was pregnant until my stomach began to swell. When Michael came out, the first thing I saw was his full head of bright reddish hair just like his father's.

Fourteen months after Michael was born, Mindy arrived. She was a little jumping bean from the first moment. She aimed to please, talkative and animated, the opposite of her brother who was like an old sage. Observing the difference, Brian predicted Michael would grow up to be a philosopher and Mindy a politician.

Michael was a thinker all right, but he thought too much and ate too little. He ate one third of the food that most babies would eat, so his weight and height were way below the average. One doctor, after observing Michael's diet pattern, told me that Michael was either too smart for his own sake or too picky to eat the food placed in front of him.

Brian hated those remarks. He shrugged off the comments and suggested another possibility. "A person's intelligence cannot be measured by what or how much he eats, especially a baby. I think Michael knows exactly what he wants in life. Food is secondary to him. That, my honey, just proves my point. Michael is not only a thinker; he thinks deep."

CHAPTER 6

Brian was a firm believer in early childhood education. He and I took turns teaching Michael and Mindy when they were only a few months old.

"But they can't read yet." I doubted the worth of our effort.

"I know," Brian patted my back with a smile, as if he was trying to explain a hard concept to his student, "but trust me, our effort is not in vain. Everything we teach them now will stimulate their brains and be deposited into their memory cells."

So English literature, poetry, Shakespeare, art, and piano were parts of their curriculum. When Mindy was almost three, she loved drawing. Her work was color-coordinated and her drawings always won her praise from the adults, even other parents and teachers.

On the contrary, Michael was not gifted in coloring, to say the least. Many times he was frustrated with crayons and he would ask me non-stop, "Mommy, why do we need so many crayons? I don't need them." I tried to explain to him that each crayon represented a color, and with different colors we could portray stories, interpret our feelings, or express our emotions.

"But I can tell stories with words. I don't need crayons." Michael insisted, with his eyes squinting in the daylight. His eyes were sensitive to light.

I was puzzled. *Mindy seems to enjoy her coloring. Why can't Michael do the same?*

I tried to explain to him, "Michael, a picture is worth a thousand words sometimes...Imaging you are telling Mommy a story with vivid pictures instead of words." I thought it was a pretty good analogy.

Michael shook his head as he replied. "But I don't need pictures to tell stories. Colors are just like words, black and white. Mommy, isn't life black and white?"

That sounded profound. *Isn't life black and white?* I don't know. Certainly in my life there was a lot of gray, how could I explain this complicated concept to a little child? It was beyond my scope.

No wonder Brian calls him a philosopher. I gave in.

"Michael, if you don't like drawing, we can do something else, like playing the piano or reading books."

His face lit up. "Mommy, can you read me the poem that Daddy read me the other night?"

I pulled him into my arms. Observing his cute little face, I asked "Michael, which poem?" I doubted he would have understood a poem. He was only five. *How can a five-year old kid appreciate poetry? Probably he confuses the Robin Hood story with a poem.*

He spoke with a joyful voice, "Remember the poem 'A Little Boy Blue' that Daddy read me? I remember the first part:

> The little toy dog is covered with dust,
> But sturdy and staunch he stands;
> And the little toy soldier is red with rust,
> And his musket moulds in his hands.
> Time was when the little toy dog was new,
> And he soldier was passing fair,

And that was the time when our Little Boy
Blue
Kissed them and put them there.

Mom, could you read me the rest?"

My eyes grew really big and my jaw almost dropped, "Michael, how…how do you memorize all those sentences? Do you understand the meaning of the words?"

"Mommy, you didn't like it?"

I suddenly realized my question must have scared him so I hugged him and softened my voice, "Oh I love it. Michael did a great job. Mommy is just wondering how you memorized the poem."

Michael looked at me, still worried about whether his answer was politically correct, "Mommy, I don't know. I just remember that you can sing that poem too."

Really? Have I ever sung that poem to Michael? Then I recalled two nights ago Brian had read Michael that poem before his bedtime. He told Michael that was one of his favorite poems when he was little for he was that "Little Boy Blue". Brian read that poem with passion, and he went to the piano and composed the music impromptu to go with the poem. Michael was so focused in listening to the lyrics that he was not aware of me standing in the background.

As my memory returned, I noticed Michael was eagerly awaiting my response.

"Oh, right, Michel, I don't have a good voice like your Daddy, but I can read it to you."

He jumped for joy. He right away gave me a big hug and a kiss. I realized I was too harsh on him. I expected Michael to have the same love for art as his sister, without giving him the liberty of defining his own.

Another memory flashed back. When Michael was three, we had taken him and Mindy to the beach, and he wrote a poem after observing the motion of the sea and its interactions with seashells. He read the poem as we took a stroll on the white sand:

> "The Seashells are the children of the Sea,
> They went to the shore to play hide and seek.
> All day long they were running, racing, laughing, and giggling,
> Forgetting time and space, they got lost in the sand.
> The Mama Sea got worried not seeing her babies,
> So she kept coming back to the shore to look for her lost kids.

"That's why the waves never stop visiting the sea shore." Michael had explained, in case we didn't understand.

I was amazed. I could only say, "Michael, that was just beautiful..."

So I shared my great findings about Michael with Brian. He was surprised to some degree, but not as shocked as I was. With a big smile, he said, "Now we have two kids. One is Picasso, and the other Shakespeare. Do you think we should work on number three, who might turn out to be Einstein one day?"

CHAPTER 7

The "dream" for child number three never came. Everything was put on hold when the doctor detected a malignant tumor inside Brian's liver. At first, Brian didn't have any symptoms except abdominal swelling and decrease in appetite. Then he felt nauseated and tired all the time. No matter how hard I pressed the need of seeing a doctor, he kept insisting it was due to many sleepless nights of research and prep work for the conference. "I just need a vacation and I will be okay." He said.

When we noticed his skin and eyes were turning yellow, Brian finally agreed to visit the hospital. After the doctor ran a variety of tests and performed the FNA biopsy, he dropped the bomb.

As soon as the words "liver cancer" flew out of the doctor's mouth, my world shattered. From that point on, Brian's condition precipitated. He became weak so quickly that he did not have the strength to joke or hug the kids or me. We witnessed his progressive deterioration in days. Smiles disappeared from Michael and Mindy's little faces. Many times I just sat in a dark corner staring at Brian, wondering if there was a light at the end of the tunnel.

"Don't give up, please. Brian, please fight the battle for me and the kids."

He opened his eyes, squeezing his last ounce of strength to smile, "Vivian, remember the poem I read you:

The mind has a thousand eyes,
And the heart but one;
Yet the light of a whole life dies
When love is done.

"Maybe God thinks I am done with love, so He is taking me away. Don't cry. I am just joking. He will take good care of you and the kids. Oh, I love all of you so much and I sometimes wish this were a bad dream. Vivian, if my mind had a thousand eyes, they would all be gazing at you. Thank you for loving me, giving me the best years of my life and the best gifts, Michael and Mindy." He reached out for my hands; once he found them, he held them so tight that his fingernails almost pierced my flesh. We stared at each other attentively and hoped our eyes would never close.

But the flesh was weak. I fell asleep.

Then I felt the grip loosen. I woke up. My back was stiff and my mouth dry. I realized Brian had slipped away, without bidding us goodbye.

Through my life up to that point, I had never had to face that kind of loss, the kind that would eat you alive. I would have lost my sanity had Michael and Mindy not been present to save it. Deep down, I would rather have been buried with Brian, but as soon as I turned and saw them, I knew I had to give them my last bit of strength.

"Vivian, you have to focus on Michael and Mindy… They are relying on you." Griping me tight, Mama wiped away my tears, as well as her own. The whole family was there grieving with me and for me. At a distance, I saw Poppa slouching, shaking his head, and sighing aloud.

So I coped. I had to be strong for the three of us. At Brian's funeral, I was as hard as a flint, as cold as ice. I lost my gravity and was totally unaware of anything or anyone around me except the big black box that held Brian. I stared at the box, not willing to let go the sight.

They dug a hole, put Brian in it, and put dirt on him. I reached out my hands to stop them, but Josh and Poppa grabbed me. They knew I would have jumped into that hole to join Brian.

So I stood there watching them shuffle dirt on him as if the dirt were poured on top of me. Then the dirt built up and turned into walls. Suddenly, the walls from four corners were closing in on me. It was I who was in the box after all. I couldn't breathe. I lost my senses. When I woke up, I realized my heart had already died, the moment Brian let go his grip…

One last time, I allowed pain to invade my heart, like hundreds of millions of termites eating me alive, slowly but surely. Then numbness, like a huge spider web, crawled all over my body, and finally shut off my senses, and my tears ran dry.

That same night I made a vow to myself that nothing was going to hurt me or make me cry again.

CHAPTER 8

A few months after Brian's passing, Michael's school called me, informing me that Michael was acting "rebelliously" in his class. I was appalled. I told the teacher that Michael would be the last person on earth to be labeled "rebellious". He just didn't own that gene. His teacher, Mrs. Ross, asked me to meet her, so we got together right after Michael's class.

"Mrs. Thompson, I think your husband's passing had a huge impact on Michael."

"Mrs. Ross, that is understandable. Michael is… Well, he was very close to his dad. But could you please be more specific about Michael's behavior?" I didn't like the sound of "rebellious", yet at the same time I tried not to offend Mrs. Ross, for she was a kind lady and Michael really liked her.

"As you know, Michael tends to be on the quiet side, which is not wrong. He kept things pretty much to himself even before Mr. Thompson passed away, but he was never rude, until two days ago. He reacted in an unexpected way."

"In what way, if I may ask?"

Mrs. Ross looked me in the eyes and said, "I cannot blame Michael one hundred percent because other kids were involved. I guess they bullied him and laughed at his drawing." Mrs. Ross was careful with her words.

I knew she was trying to be impartial and I appreciated her effort. "How did Michael react to that?"

"He took crayons to those kids' desks and drew lines and circles across their papers. Basically he ruined their drawings. Not only that, Michael yelled something improper at one of the kids."

"Michael never yelled at anyone!" I was so shocked that I didn't know what else to say.

Mrs. Ross pulled me aside and explained. "Michael told the boy that his father was going to 'abandon' him and his family'. It was not a nice thing to say to a classmate, whether it is true or not?"

Michael said what? There is no way Michael could have said that.

Michael knew more words than most of the same age kids, because Brian had always stressed learning. Brian started teaching Michael Shakespeare when he was two. So I had no doubt that Michael knew the meaning of the verb "Abandon", but that was not the point. The point was he could not have said those things. I shook my head, trying to make sense of it.

"Mrs. Ross, there must have been some misunderstanding. You know Michael well; he would have never said those things to others. He just doesn't have any rudeness in him."

"Mrs. Thompson, that is why it stunned me as well. If I had not been there and heard Michael's words, I would have never believed it." Mrs. Ross shook her head. She knew how I felt and she didn't know what else to do to make me feel better. "I also contacted those kids' parents about their unkind behavior toward Michael so they were not excused either. But I have to let you know as well. After that incident, Michael refused to draw anything that I assigned the class, and when I asked him the reason, he simply said that he didn't know how to draw it."

"Mrs. Ross, what was your assignment for the class?"

"Oh, I asked the class to draw a rainbow."

"A rainbow?" I thought to myself that would be an easy assignment. Even Mindy drew her first rainbow as young as two. "Did you ask for a special kind of rainbow? Did Michael say anything else after you asked him?"

Mrs. Ross thought for a moment. "The assignment was to draw their rainbow with their seven favorite colors. When Michael told me he did not know how to draw it, I told him it was very easy and he just needed to pick any seven colors. He then told me something very odd…"

"What did he say?" I almost stuttered.

"He said his rainbow only has two colors." Mrs. Ross looked at me intensely, hoping I could somehow make sense out of this answer and explained it to her.

"Mrs. Ross, I am so sorry that Michael made trouble in your class. I know Michael has eye problems, and it was our intention to take him to see an eye specialist, but then Brian got ill.

"I don't know what to say but I will find out why Michael acted weirdly." I felt my heart suddenly torn into many pieces.

She patted me on the back, and gave me a hug. "Mrs. Thompson, I know raising two kids by yourself is not easy. You are doing your very best. Michael is the most brilliant kid I have ever taught. I just hope his father's passing will not hinder his learning."

I nodded as I fought back my emotions. I didn't want to show any weakness. "I will keep in close touch, Mrs. Ross. Thank you for contacting me."

Mrs. Ross nodded as she walked out of the classroom.

Michael ran to me as soon as he saw us wrapping up the conversation. He gave me a kiss on the cheek and a big bear hug. That was the kind of hug he used to give his Daddy. They would spread out their arms wide and straight and they embrace each other tight and close. That meant complete trust between buddies.

"Michael, so sorry that you've waited for a long time." I said.

Squinting his eyes as he looked up, Michael smiled as he replied, "Mommy, you know while I was sitting under the tree waiting for you, the sun was setting and its light splashed all over me. It felt so good. I opened my palms and captured the light. Do you want to see the light in my palms?" Michael showed me his hands. His cheeks were glowing with a reddish tan, which accented his fair skin and red hair.

I touched his face; it was still warm. I smiled, "So you got me the sunshine?" I was surprised that Michael had enjoyed playing in the sun. He was not a big fan of the daylight because of his sensitive eyes.

Showing me the light in his hands, Michael lowered his face, "Mommy, do I have to take the drawing class? I don't really like it." I couldn't see his face so I scooped down to his height. "Michael, how come? Did someone give you a hard time?"

He was quiet. I did not want to press this issue right at that moment so I stood up and walked with him.

"Mommy, did you ever see a rainbow?"

"Yah! You did too, right? Remember the other day we were running in the rain, we saw it together with Daddy. It was like a bridge across the sky." This was the subject I wanted to get into.

"Mommy, how come Mrs. Ross asked us to draw the rainbow with seven colors?" Michael lifted up his face looking at me.

I kept walking for I wanted to make it as casual as possible. "Michael, can you tell Mommy how many colors are in your rainbow?"

"There are only two. And it has always been two."

"Two colors? What are those two colors, Michael? "

"Dark and light, Mommy."

I pressed on, "You mean black and white."

"And shades in between." Michael said.

"Michael, but do you remember you read me the poem "Little Boy Blue?" What about the color of blue?" I was searching my memory to come up with something that would show any sign of colors.

"Mommy, that just means someone is sad." He was certain.

After picking up Mindy, we went to Brian's grave to talk to him. It was a kind of ritual for them to remember their Daddy, even though I was not certain how much that would mean to them when they had grown up, but they insisted on going there often. While we were there, I would clean up the gravesite while Michael and Mindy would sit down in front of the tombstone, sharing their day with their dad.

Michael loved to read stories like "the Little Prince" to his dad with Mindy singing songs in the background. I tried to listen to Michael with one ear and Mindy with the other.

Mindy ran to me and jumped up on my back, "Mommy, do you like my singing?"

I turned to hug her and tickle her. "Of course I love it! You have the most beautiful voice. Remember, Daddy said that all the time!"

She was giggling and laughing. Then Michael joined us in tickling and laughing.

I could feel Brian was laughing with three of us, at a distance.

CHAPTER 9

Michael was a night owl. His eyes came alive at night. After putting Mindy to bed, I sneaked into his room, dimmed the light a little, and tried to have a heart-to-heart conversation with Michael about the incident in Mrs. Ross's class.

"Michael, do you remember, when Daddy was with us we promised each other that we would always tell the truth?"

Michael nodded. "Mommy, I always do." He seemed pretty sure that he had held his end of the promise.

I touched his soft hair as I nodded. "I believe you. You have always been a good boy, and your Daddy and I are very proud of you. You know that, right?"

Michael nodded again. He then sensed my upcoming questions. "Yes, Mommy."

I tried to set my voice in a non-accusatorial tone, "Michael, you know Mommy had a conversation with Mrs. Ross this afternoon about what had happened two days ago in your art class. Do you remember what happened?"

Michael turned quiet. I waited. I knew my son.

"Mommy, Tom and two other boys came to my desk pretending to borrow my crayons, and as soon as they saw my drawing, they started laughing at me. Mommy, it was not the first time they had laughed at my drawings, but I had never said anything. Tom and the boys said they had never seen any painting worse than mine and it would have won the contest if there was an award for the worst drawing." Michael looked down at the bed sheet.

I wanted to hug him and let the whole ordeal go, but I had to stay strong to get to the bottom of it, so I continued pressing the question, "So what happened after that? Did you return the favor and do something that you shouldn't have?"

Michael looked up at my face, searching my eyes. "Mommy, they first called me blind, and then called me an orphan because Daddy had died. And they said Daddy was an old man that married a young chick. Mommy, are they talking about you? Are you the young chick? I don't like the way they talked about you."

Seeing tears forming in his eyes, I couldn't help but hold him in my arms. "Michael, they were being mean. You are not blind, and you are not an orphan. That was not something nice for them to say." I couldn't come up with any other sentences to condemn them. Deep down I knew it had a lot to do with their upbringing. Tom's father was notorious for his explosive temper and abusive behavior at home, but I was not sure whether I should convey that info to Michael.

If Brian were here… He would have the right words to say and wisdom to handle this.

I touched Michael's little face as I searched for words. "Michael, your Daddy was indeed older than Mommy, but the age gap didn't stop us from loving each other and we loved each other very much. The way Tom presented it was not proper, and I know Mrs. Ross would have disciplined him had she known about the conversation between you two. You are not blind, nor are you an orphan. Don't ever believe that. Mommy is still here and Mommy will never let you become an orphan, not you or Mindy. That is a promise."

Michael nodded. He allowed me to wipe away his tears, but I was not done. "Mrs. Ross told me that you did something equally not nice to Tom and the other two boys. Is it true?"

Michael bit his lip. He looked down and then looked up. He said very sadly, "Mommy, they took my crayons and painted my paper all over. They pushed me, and kept laughing and calling me bad names, so I got mad. I ran to their desks and did the same thing they did to my drawing. Mommy, I am so sorry. I shouldn't have done that, but I was very angry."

"Did you say something to Tom about his dad?"

Michael replied without any hesitation, "Yes, I did. I told him his Daddy was going to abandon him and his family."

"Michael, why did you say those unkind words? Didn't Daddy and Mommy teach you better than that?" I was dumbfounded. That was not like him.

Michael lowered his head. I knew he was contrite, so I suggested a possibility, "Did you try to get back at Tom, so you said those hurtful words?"

Michael shook his head. "No, Mommy, I just told him the truth. His dad is going to leave him and his family for someone else—"

"Michael, you don't know that for a fact. His dad has shown no sign of leaving him or his family. Anything untrue is called rumor, and we shouldn't spread rumors."

"Mommy, it is not a rumor. It is going to happen soon." Michael looked innocent as he said those words.

"How do you know it is going to happen? Did someone break the news to you?" I asked, shaking my head in disbelief.

Michael wanted to say something but he swallowed it. He lowered his eyelids. I could no longer see his eyes. I waited for his reply, but Michael was quiet with his head hung low, so I assumed he must have felt badly for what he had done. "Michael, we all make mistakes. I know you acted out of anger and frustration. Sometimes when we are under attack, we just want to hurl hurtful words back at the person who hurts us."

Michael still remained silent. He slowly shook his head.

"Do you want to say something?"

He shook his head, without even looking at me. I interpreted his silence as being remorseful. Looking at the clock next to his bed, I realized it was past his bedtime, so I tried to wrap up the conversation. "Michael, I love you and that will never change. You know that, right?"

Michael then looked up, searching for my eyes and seeking confirmation. He nodded. "Mommy, I love you too. I am going to take care of you all my life, even when you are old in the wheelchair," He said.

I touched his little face and couldn't help but think of Brian. They had such a resemblance in their eyes, noses and lips. I heaved a sigh.

"You are thinking of Daddy." Michael said.

I was surprised that Michael could read my mind, but I didn't want to hide my feelings from him, I nodded.

Michael then crawled unto my laps and rested his head there. "Mommy, I am sorry that I brought you troubles. I won't do that again."

Fighting back tears, I touched Michael's hair, allowing my fingers to stroll up and down his soft curls. Then he fell asleep on my lap.

CHAPTER 10

I took Michael to an ophthalmologist who had a lab inside his clinic. When we were called in, the doctor looked at me and smiled. "Mrs. Thompson, I think I knew your husband. He was my college professor Brian Thompson. Is that right? How is he doing? Is he well?"

I took a deep breath. "Dr. Field, we lost him to cancer a few months ago."

His eyes sank into a black hole. "I am so sorry to hear that. He was one of my favorite professors. Because of the conviction he had, I almost changed my career to become a politician. He taught us to think outside the box, to challenge the stale status quo polices that were destroying our society. That probably was the most valuable lesson that I got in college."

I thanked him for his kind words. "Dr. Field, I don't know whether you are the right person to help me solve this puzzle of my son. You see, Michael somehow cannot grasp or comprehend the concept of 'color'. For instance, he squints a lot, claims that a rainbow only consists of two colors, and he gets frustrated with many different crayon colors. Does this sound normal to you?" I probably sounded foolish but I didn't care. I needed to get to the bottom of this.

Michael was sitting in a room across from us, occupied with lots of toys around him.

"Do you mind my taking a look at your son's eyes? What is his name again? By the way, he reminded me of Professor Thompson—handsome, skinny and with a full head of bright red hair." He smiled as he looked over at Michael.

"His name is Michael. Thank you for your compliment."

Dr. Field turned toward Michael's direction and said, "Michael, do you mind coming over here? I have more toys here. Do you see this stuffed animal in my hand? His name is Jimmy. I think Jimmy wants to meet you."

Dr. Field waved a little toy dog at Michael. Michael ran in to the room.

"Michael, how old are you? Do you have sisters or brothers or dogs or cats at home?"

Michael politely answered Dr. Field, but his eyes were riveted upon the stuffed animal. "I am five. I have a younger sister. Her name is Mindy. We don't have pets yet but I hope one day we can get a dog—" He glanced at me to get an approval.

I smiled.

Dr. Field handed the toy to Michael. As Michael gave a hug to the dog, Dr. Field asked a question. "Michael, so you do like dogs. Do you like Jimmy? Obviously Jimmy likes you. You are such a good boy. By the way, can you tell me what color Jimmy is?"

Michael was holding the toy very gently. He had asked for a little puppy in the past, but Brian was allergic to pets so we had never gotten one.

"Jimmy is dark color. He is probably black. He is so much like the puppy next door, isn't he, Mommy?"

Dr. Field and I exchanged glances. We both knew Jimmy was red.

Dr. Field walked away for a few minutes. His assistant informed me that he was preparing some medical tests to use to examine Michael's eyes.

Dr. Field came back. He sat next to Michael watching him play. He chatted with Michael and waited until the right moment. "Michael, I can see you really like Jimmy. You want to take him home?"

"Oh no, Dr. Field, I can't. Jimmy is yours." Michael returned the stuffed animal to Dr. Field. He knew he must not covet any toys unless they came from Brian or me. We had stressed that rule numerous times.

Dr. Field smiled, "Don't worry. Your mother won't object to it. But before you say yea or nay, I want you to help me with something that is not too hard. Can you do that for me?"

Michael looked over at me for approval. I nodded, so he nodded to Dr. Field.

"Thank you very much, Michael. I have to take a closer look at your eyes and run some tests on you. I promise they won't hurt. Is that all right?"

Michael nodded again, so Dr. Field held his little hand and they entered to the lab. I did not know how he was going to do it, but I felt comfortable with him, especially witnessing his patience with Michael. I also knew had Michael not felt comfortable with Dr. Field, he would have asked for my company. He was cautious for his age.

I didn't know how much time had elapsed, and I started to get worried, so I went to Dr. Field's assistant to make sure everything was all right. She checked on them and assured me that things were under control.

Then the lab door opened. Michael ran out first, followed by Dr. Field. Michael was still holding Jimmy. He looked tired, especially his eyes. Dr. Field looked stressed. I stood up and he signaled me to sit down.

"Do you want my assistant to take Michael to the playroom?"

I thought it was unnecessary. Michael was pretty mature for his age, and he had the right to know what was going on with his eyes, so I gave Dr. Field a signal to go ahead.

"Mrs. Thompson, I did some tests on Michael's eyes and found something unusual."

"Yes, Dr. Field. You have my undivided attention."

"First off, I don't want to sound alarming." He tried to smile but failed.

"Please go ahead." I looked at him straight in the eyes.

"Michael is color-blind."

"Color-blind? You mean he cannot differentiate between red and green or some other color combinations?" I recalled something called color-blindness in my Biology class. Color-blind people tend to have problems with driving for they can't tell a red light from a green light. That was as far as my knowledge stretched.

"Michael sees no color except black and white. He has a condition called Achromatopsia or Rod Monochromacy, i.e. the inability to see color due to absence or no function of the cone cells.

"You see, our human eyes have this light sensitive tissue called retina that contains two types of cells, the rods and the cones. Rods function mainly in dim light and provide black-and-white vision, while cones support daytime vision and the perception of color. Therefore, if the cone cells are absent or nonfunctioning, a person like Michael is not only sensitive to daylight or bright light but also is deprived of the vision of color."

He stopped for a moment to see if he had lost me, but then continued without hesitation, "Color Agnosia or Cerebral Achromatopsia might be caused by damage to the brain, physical trauma, hemorrhage, tumor tissue growth or even mutation of the gene—Mrs. Thompson, are you all right?"

"What? Achro...What is the name again?" My jaw dropped and my head spun. *Does that mean Michael was born abnormal or could turn blind one day? What did Dr. Field say about a tumor growing in the brain?* I suddenly got light-headed. I gave Dr. Filed a blank look as if he were speaking in a foreign language.

Dr. Field fetched me a glass of water. He then sat down before me and stared at me as he spoke, "Mrs. Thompson, are you okay? This is a very rare form of color blindness that accounts for 1 in every 30,000 to 40,000 cases in America, but I have not met one person in real life.

"Having said that, I want to stress that people out there are sharing the same symptom. Michael is not alone. In fact, in the Pohnpei state including the island of Pingelap in the Pacific Ocean, more than five percent of its population are born with Achromatopsia."

I mumbled to myself in disbelief, "But Michael wasn't born there. Why does he share their vision? Did

I do something wrong when I was pregnant with him? Was it due to some over-the-counter medicine I took during pregnancy? I don't recall Brian mentioning that he was colorblind. Why do people on this island have this condition?" I turned to Dr. Field, "Is this reversible?"

"Mrs. Thompson, no. It is no one's fault. Known genetic causes of this condition are mutations of the cone cell. You see, back in 1775, if my memory serves me right, a catastrophic typhoon swept through the island and killed almost ninety percent of the population, leaving twenty people or so. It was believed that one of the survivors, namely Nahnmwarki Mwanenised, who was the ruler at the time, was a carrier for complete achromatopsia.

"Even though it was a recessive genetic condition, yet due to heavy inbreeding, it now boasts a much higher ratio than the rest of the world. The local people called the condition 'Maskun' which means 'Not-See' in their language. As far as I know, there is no cure as yet, but there are treatments."

Michael was next to me. He waited for his turn to speak. First he took my hand, "Mommy, what is color-blind? Is color-blind a handicap?"

That word "handicap" struck right at my stomach. I turned to him, "No, Michael, you are not handicapped and never will be."

"Mommy, that's okay. At least we can park at the handicap spot so you don't need to walk too far to my class or to the grocery store." Michael looked at me in a serious manner.

I then was engulfed by tidal waves of emotions. We had been worried about him and his eyes all along, and yet he was worried about my parking space. I grabbed Michael and hugged him tight.

Dr. Field patted my back and touched Michael's head. He waited until I let go of Michael. "Mrs. Thompson, you have a great son and you should be proud of him." Then he turned to Michael and said to him, "You do not have a handicap, and don't let anyone tell you that, even at school. I have to do more research to find out what treatment suits your situation the best. Are you okay with that?"

Michael nodded.

I thanked him for his time and effort, but was still disoriented and confounded.

As we were leaving Dr. Field's office, Dr. Field walked us to the door. He was quiet until the moment we said good-bye. "Mrs. Thompson, I don't know if it is appropriate, but may I call you sometime?" Dr. Field asked. He was blushing.

Thinking he wanted to discuss Michael's situation, I absentmindedly nodded my head. "Of course. You can call us anytime."

He shook my hand and saw us off.

We walked toward the car, which was parked a few streets away. We held hands tightly but said nothing until we got into the car.

"Mommy, I miss Daddy. Do you?" Michael squinted at the glow of the setting sun.

I looked at him, wondering what he saw in the sunset. *Does Michael see what I see in the sky? Does he see any colors, a spectrum of glaring colors that I couldn't even narrate with earthly words? Or does he just perceive black ink randomly splashed on a huge piece of white canopy like Chinese Calligraphy? How much has he missed out in life?*

"Yes, I miss him very much too." I replied. *Oh yes, I wish Brian were here telling me everything would be okay. I wish I had his wisdom and calmness to deal with challenges and find positive answers for life. I miss his broad shoulders that I leaned on.*

CHAPTER 11

Brian's insurance policy could only sustain us for so long, so I applied for work through an employment agency. After a few weeks, they notified me a medical company might grant me an interview, and the good news was that they weren't opposed to working with someone like me who needed flexible hours.

I was excited about the prospect, but I was torn between work and family. I desperately needed a job to put food on the table, but at the same time I wondered if I could cope with the pressure of serving as single mom and working woman.

With all the worries forming in the back of my mind, I decided to take Michael and Mindy to church on that Sunday. I don't know why, but I felt an impelling urge to go to a church.

Through a postcard in the mail, we had heard of a church located in between Los Angeles and Santa Monica. As we walked to the door, the greeters warmly invited us in. They noted we were new, so they showed us around. Mindy insisted on attending the Sunday School to play with similar age kids. The Sunday school teachers were very kind, so I felt at ease leaving Mindy with them, after Mindy assured me that she would not boss the teachers and the class around, I smiled and gave her a kiss on the cheek.

I turned to Michael, who was holding my hand, suggesting he pick a Sunday School class that suited him.

"Mommy, could I go with you? I promise I will sit tight and not bother you." We walked into the Sanctuary and picked the seats in the second row from the back, just in case we had to exit early.

The worship songs were moving. However, I didn't feel like singing, so I stared at the screen the whole time trying to comprehend the words. Michael stood quietly next to me. Then the pastor walked in. He gestured us to sit down.

The pastor began his sermon with a question. "If anyone of you in the audience has never encountered any troubles whatsoever in life since the moment you were born, and you have had a perfect smooth sailing journey thus far, please raise your hand, so we can see who you are and admire you. We, i.e. the rest of us, really yearn to, long to, and aspire to learn your secrets. And if you don't mind sharing it, could we please move in to your house to live with you so we can learn first-hand?"

The audience chuckled. No one raised hands.

Then the pastor corrected himself. "I might have scared those people by saying that we all want to move in with them. So please allow me to scratch that part. Please just raise your hands so we can admire you."

The audience laughed louder. I looked around. Still, no one raised his or her hand.

The pastor cleared his voice and then said, "So I guess it is a fair assumption that life is no bed of roses. But if anyone of you desires to challenge this statement, you still have a chance to speak up at this final moment, or forever hold your peace."

Where is he going with this? I thought to myself.

"That's why Jesus told us in John 16:33 that 'in this world you will have trouble.' He didn't say you might have trouble, but you will have trouble. It is guaranteed that you and I will face troubles in life; some more while others less.

"Not only is our life not perfect, but you and I are not perfect either. So we are looking at a world that is imperfect because it is made of imperfect people like you and me, and the truth is that we are part of the problem, not the solution.

"When God created men in His image on the sixth day, He purposed to have an intimate relationship with them. He commanded men to multiply and manage His creation. Once sin entered the world, through the devil's temptation and men's reception, the bond between God and men was shattered. Crimes, vices, and the big sting, death ensued. God had to kick men out of His garden because man violated His trust. At the same time, God knew He had to initiate a 'Savings Plan' in order to bring His lost people back to Him, or else the whole human race would be forever doomed, and ultimately exterminated.

"Every one of us was and is under the heavy yoke of sin. We've all sinned. Sin is anything that causes us to offend God or displease Him, such as our imperfect thoughts or deeds. Since God is perfect and holy, anything imperfect or unholy offends Him. It maybe our lying tongues, our impure or selfish motives, covetousness, lustful thoughts, or simply nodding your head to the least of harm or shutting your eyes to the least of good."

So where is hope then? I suddenly regretted taking Michael with me. *His already philosophical mind is going to be overloaded.*

Somehow the pastor read my mind. He looked around the audience and said, "I know what you are thinking. You are thinking that there is no hope, then."

He stopped for a moment and then said, "The Good News is that Jesus never gives up on us. After He told us in this world we will have trouble, He also said 'but take heart! I have overcome the world.' What a outrageous claim Jesus has made!"

"Overcome the world? That means Jesus not only has overcome your struggles and heartaches caused by the imperfect world, He has also overcome your imperfection by forgiving your sin and making you whole, if you allow Him to.

"We humans can never save ourselves from God's wrath, nor are we able to reach heaven by our own effort or merit. So God reached down to us by sending His one and only begotten Son Jesus Christ to walk the earth to bridge the gap, so we would have the up-close look at God Himself, the first-hand account of God's Word, which renders Truth and Hope.

"Not only that, God had to send His Son, perfect, with no sin, to Calvary to trade places with sinners like you and me. Jesus suffered the most excruciating pain not for His own sake but for us. He shed blood and died on the cross to pay for our sins, so we can be saved from the eternal condemnation of God's wrath, and reconciled with God the Father in Heaven. My friend, that's Love with the capital L."

The pastor stopped, overcome with emotion. After a few seconds, he resumed his sermon.

"Have you felt life has scourged you non-stop? Have you felt lonely at times or wanted to throw a pity-party for yourself? Have you felt the world had abandoned or betrayed you so that no one would even shed a tear for you if you die tonight? Have you wondered if things could ever get better, because everywhere you turn, there is doom and gloom? Have you been struck by a tragedy or a calamity that cut you so deep that you thought you would never recover? Have you felt such darkness lurking on your back that you would never see the light? Have you ever doubted why you were born and the purpose of your life?"

The message grabbed my heart. It was totally in sync with my contending passions. Ever since Brian's passing, I had been sucked into a black hole. I tried to climb out of it, but the storm kept knocking me down and pushing me back. I tried to stand, but the rage of the wind would not grant me a footing. I wanted to scream, but no voice was uttered.

I finally rent the dark veil and escaped, bolting at full speed. My sweat broke out and drenched my whole body. My brain ran short of oxygen but I didn't care; I kept running. In exhaustion I reached the finish line, just to find out it was my starting point. I was back to the heart of the black hole. I wanted to sob my heart out but as I turned, I found Michael and Mindy reaching out for me. I so desired to give them my very best, but everything I offered was leftovers, leftovers from my drained body and soul…

"Help me! Help me! Someone out there help me," My heart screamed.

Suddenly I was pulled out of my trance. Realizing Michael was sitting right next me, I turned and saw him listening attentively, with his back upright, eyes looking straight at the pastor.

I turned back to the pastor.

"Jesus didn't walk the earth to win the Nobel Peace Prize or receive the Bob Hope Humanitarian Award, but for you and me, blood for blood and flesh for flesh. He took our filthy place and gave us His righteousness. He was born to walk the loneliest journey from Bethlehem to the cross for you and for me.

"Can you imagine the purpose of someone's life being to die for you so you can live? He lay down Himself, the perfect Lamb of God, on the burning altar as the perfect sacrifice to atone for our sin so we too can become the sons and daughters of God.

"Jesus came to the earth to find you and to carry your burden because He has seen all your weariness and exhaustion. He heard your cry and saw your tears. He is offering His hand to reach for you, and as soon as you grab His hand, your heavy burden will roll off, and your soul will find peace and rest in Him."

While we were bowing our heads, praying, with the music in the background, the pastor said, "If any one of you with a heavy heart wants Jesus to lift it, or any one of you has something troubling you so deeply that you have been seeking answers from heaven, come forward now to the pulpit so I can pray for you and Jesus will help you. Ask and it will be given to you; seek and you will find; knock and the door will be open to you. Just come."

My eyes were closed, my heart was racing, and my mind went blank as I pondered how the pastor knew my feelings. I don't remember how long it lasted, but finally the music stopped. I opened my eyes. Michael's seat was empty. I looked down and around but could not find him.

I panicked. Grabbing my purse, I was about to rush outside to call 911. All of a sudden a hand grabbed me. It belonged to an old lady sitting two seats from my left.

She said, "Look! Your boy is up yonder."

Then her index finger, in slow motion, magically and poetically pointed toward the front of the church and then up to the pulpit.

I saw Michael's little figure standing right next to the pastor on the platform with six adults. I had to close my mouth really quickly or else I would have screamed.

What on earth is Michael up there with the pastor and other grown-ups? Where did he get the courage to get up there? Can he really comprehend what the pastor said about heavy burdens and weary hearts? But those things were meant for adults. He is too young to grasp that concept, plus he is so shy.

On the one hand I was embarrassed, for I felt many eyes looking at me, but on the other hand, I was amused to see his little figure up there in the midst of all the tall adults.

The pastor asked for their names, introduced them and prayed for them individually in a low voice so the audience would not hear. I was still in disbelief that Michael was up there. It seemed a hundred years had elapsed before the service concluded. I raced against the flow of people to approach the pulpit, and at the same time tried to avoid all the glances hurled my way. When I finally reached the pulpit, Michael saw me and smiled. "Mommy, now we will be okay. Jesus is going to help us."

I squeezed out a smile.

The pastor standing next to Michael welcomed me. His smile was warm and genuine. Shaking his hand but ignoring his moving lips, I said, "Pastor, I am so sorry. I did not know Michael was going to come forward. When I found out, it was too late."

He then replied with the same genuine smile. "Please call me Franklin. In one of the Bible recorded events, Jesus' disciples tried to block the children from coming to Him, but He stopped them from doing so, for He loved children. He even said to His disciples, 'unless you change and become like little children, you will never enter the kingdom of heaven.' Therefore, whoever humbles himself like this child is the greatest in the kingdom of heaven.

"Michael is God's child and is precious in God's sight. In fact, we should all learn from him per the Lord's command. I am proud of him being brave and coming forward."

I was touched by his sincerity, yet I questioned his capability of understanding my trials and heartaches. Lip service was the easy part, so I politely thanked him for his insight. Using picking up Mindy as an excuse,

I grabbed Michael's hand, and fled as fast as possible from the pastor's sight.

I felt I was running from something, something that I couldn't put my finger on.

As soon as we picked up Mindy, I took them straight to the car. Once we got in, I asked, "Michael, why did you go to the pulpit?"

"Mommy, I felt this *tug* on my heart to go when Pastor Franklin called. He was calling anyone who has a heavy burden on his heart and is troubled."

"Do you have a heavy burden or a troubled heart?" I asked.

Michael answered me without hesitation. "No, but you do, Mommy. I could feel it, and I knew Jesus was calling me, so I went."

"So did you ask the pastor to pray for your eyes?"

"Mommy, I asked Pastor Franklin to pray that you will be happy and never worry again. I also asked Jesus to take care of Daddy since Daddy is up there with him. Then I asked Jesus to take care of you, Mindy, and all of us."

I was speechless. I became teary-eyed but I quickly blinked them dry. I didn't want my kids to see their mother cry. I wanted them to know even if the sky were to fall they could rely on their mother to protect them.

Mindy spoke from the back seat. "I know Jesus, too. Mommy, listen to me. I can sing the Jesus Loves Me song.

Jesus loves me this I know,
For the Bible tells me so...
La-la-la-la-la...

La-la-la-la. He is strong.

Oh Jesus loves me, Oh Jesus loves me, Oh Jesus loves me,

For Bible tells me so."

I listened to her cute voice and could not stop smiling. Sometimes she would sing a whole song with hundreds of "La la las" and then follow with the questions "What do you think? Do you like my song?" Michael often asked Mindy the name of the song and Mindy would shrug her shoulders and answer, "I don't know, and I don't care— but do you like my song?"

At those precious moments, I would let go my sense of reality and join them in being silly. I knew that was what Brian would have done.

When Brian came to mind, I always felt this deep scar in my heart. On the one hand, I loved him so much that I was still in denial of his passing, while on the other I blamed him for my grief. Then I became quiet and depressed. I fought back all the memories and moved on.

I can't afford to let down of my guard. I can't afford to be defeated. Michael and Mindy are relying on me. I have to be strong for the three of us.

CHAPTER 12

A couple of days later, we got a call from someone from Brian's past.

Michael answered the phone while I was giving Mindy a bath. I rushed out to see Michael holding the phone and carrying on a conversation so I asked him who was calling.

"It is the other grandma," Michael answered.

What other grandma? I shook my head. *There is only one grandma.*

I took over the phone, "This is Vivian. Mama, is that you?" Then there was a dead silence from the phone for a few seconds.

"Hello? Hello? This is Vivian." I was getting a little impatient. It couldn't be Mama. *Is someone playing a joke on us?* So I spoke louder. "This is Mrs. Thompson speaking. Who is this?"

"Hel-low. I was Mrs. Thompson once myself."

I was stunned. "You are?"

"Call me Colleen. That is my first name. I prefer it," she answered.

Colleen was Brian's Mom's name. "Colleen, is this really you? How are you doing? How did you get our number?"

"Your name is Vivian, right? I just heard about Brian. That's why I am flying to the States tomorrow. Do you mind if I stop by and visit you? If you don't want me to, I understand, but please allow me to at least visit Brian's resting place. Please."

My heart was torn into pieces. How could I turn down a grieving mother's wish?

"Yes, you are welcome to visit us anytime." I answered. However, the stories that Brian had told me about his mother flashed back. I wondered had Brian been alive, would he have welcomed his mother with open arms? I didn't know the answer, but somehow I felt I was obligated to do so.

Colleen arrived two days after our phone conversation. We went to the airport to pick her up. She had told me she would be wearing a navy blue suit, but as soon as we got to the airport I realized it was common business attire so I panicked that I wouldn't be able to recognize her. The moment she walked out of the Immigration/Customs area, though, I knew it was Colleen, for I saw Brian in her. Michael and Mindy waved at her, and she approached us with a smile. She gave me a hug, and then took turns hugging Michael and Mindy.

"Vivian, they are so beautiful. They must have taken the best from Brian and you. I have talked with Michael on the phone, but was not introduced to this beautiful young lady. What's your name?"

Mindy was very flattered at being called beautiful. She giggled and hugged Colleen back, "My name is Sleeping Beauty, because I like to sleep. Are you the other Grandma?"

"Yes, my dear Sleeping Beauty. You can call me Grandma." Colleen kissed Mindy on the cheek. She then pulled two beautiful dolls from her bag and handed them to Mindy.

She smiled and said to Mindy, "I hope you like these two dolls. They left their home in Paris, and hopped on a plane with Grandma, so they can live with you."

Mindy's eyes popped. She smiled from ear to ear. She climbed up on Colleen to express her gratitude.

"Grandma, do you want to hear the story about Sleeping Beauty? Do you know she fell asleep for one hundred years, until the prince showed up?"

Michael said, "Grandma, my sister's name is Mindy. Sleeping Beauty is her nickname."

Colleen then turned to Michael, "So what's your nickname, Michael?"

"My Daddy called me his Little Prince. It is from a story book."

"You must love books just as your Daddy did when he was little. I brought you quite a few books that used to belong to your Daddy." Colleen opened her luggage to show Michael all the books.

Michael's face lit up. He turned to me and asked, "Mommy, can I have them? They are Daddy's old books."

I nodded. How could I say no? Michael was on the top of the world. Observing Colleen being so gentle and loving, and her getting along with Michael and Mindy so well, I wondered whether I had misjudged her? Was it right for me to blame her for abandoning Brian at such a young age?

The pastor's message from the past Sunday suddenly said in my ear that we were living in an imperfect world. We were part of the problem. *So what right do I have to judge her?* I felt obliged to give her the benefit of the doubt.

We took Colleen to Brian's grave. She brought a bunch of flowers and placed them in front of Brian's tombstone. Michael, Mindy, and I waited in a distance. I told them to respect their Grandmother's private time with Daddy. They had not seen each other for a long time and they had a lot to catch up on.

"Mommy, how come we've never heard from this Grandma before? Did she not like Daddy?" Michael leaned his head on my waist.

"Mommy, I like this Grandma. Do you think she can stay with us, forever?" Mindy leaned on me from the other side. I knew Mindy was really impressed by Colleen and her dolls. Brian and I had never been big believers in spoiling our children with toys, and now Colleen showed up with two gorgeous ones.

I smiled at both of them. "Michael, I believe Grandma loved your Daddy just as much as I love you. There must be some odd reason that they couldn't see each other. Mindy, why don't you ask Grandma that question! I think she will be very happy learning of your hospitality."

"What's Horse-Bill-T?" Mindy asked.

"It means you are generous and kind to Grandma. You treat her very nice," Michael said without correcting her pronunciation.

After a while, Colleen walked toward us. Her eyes were wet. Mindy took her handkerchief from her pocket and handed it to her. Colleen squeezed out a smile, but we all knew she was not in the mood to talk, so we kept quiet on the way home.

While I was cooking dinner, Colleen came down to the kitchen to help me. Her eyes were still swollen.

"Vivian, thank you for taking time off to accompany me, and I am sorry about the short notice of the visit."

I stopped stirring the soup and turned to face her, "Colleen, you are welcome and no trouble at all. In fact, Mindy wanted to ask you whether you might want to stay with us, forever?" I hoped that would cheer her up.

"Really? I love them, both Michael and Mindy. They are great kids. Brian must have been very proud of them, as I was…" Colleen gave me a hug.

I wanted to ask her about the past but I was not brave enough. I didn't know where to start, or how to put words in the right order. Should I start with, "If you were so proud of Brian, why did you abandon him?" or, "Do you know you hurt Brian so much that he was afraid of having relations with women for many years? How could you do this to your own son?" But either way would have come out wrong.

Right before nine o'clock, I signaled Michael and Mindy about their bedtime by pointing at the clock. They were having fun playing with dolls and reading the books given by their Grandma. I didn't want to spoil their fun, but I knew they had school the next day, so I insisted on their rest.

Mindy said, "Mommy, can Grandma take us to bed?"

Michael didn't object, so I kissed them good night. I finished the chores while Colleen walked them to their rooms. After I was done with cleaning, I went to their rooms to check the light. I heard Michael's voice.

"Grandma, I saw the book you gave Daddy. You drew a heart and inside the heart you wrote:

To my most precious Little Prince Brian,

May this book unlock the gateway to your future kingdom!

Little Prince is also my nickname from Daddy."

"I know. You told me earlier. I remember." Colleen's voice showed a deep affection toward Michael.

"Grandma, why did you leave Daddy when he was little? You didn't love him any more?" He shot out his question without any warning sign.

There was a long pause. I sensed the clock was ticking, and I felt sorry for Coleen, so I stepped into the room.

"Michael, it is kind of late. Grandma should get some rest. You need to go to school tomorrow as well. Mindy is already asleep."

Colleen said, "No, it is quite all right. I am glad Michael asked the question. Vivian, did Brian think that I had abandoned him?" She turned to me.

I didn't see anger in her eyes but sadness. I nodded.

"So until Brian drew his last breadth, he still held that view against me. Is that right?" Colleen looked me straight in the eyes.

I nodded again. Colleen sighed. She lowered her head.

Michael crawled next to me and placed one hand on Colleen's shoulder. "Grandma, I don't mean to make you sad. I am sorry."

But I knew Michael didn't rip open the scars. The wounds bled because it had never healed.

Then Colleen faced up to me, "Vivian, please tell me more."

I hesitated for a few seconds. Then I told her about Brian's sadness because of her departure, and his great disappointment when he flew to Paris to visit her.

Colleen's eyes turned big as she listened to me. She looked confused at times, searching for answers while at other times she seemed totally lost in her train of thoughts. Toward the end of the story, she forced a smile.

I stopped. I noticed Michael's head was on my lap. He looked at me and then at Colleen. We both were waiting for her reaction.

"What has he done? What has he done to Brian and me?" Colleen bit her lip to stop her tears from falling, but the attempt failed. I handed her a tissue.

Colleen lowered her head in her hands, sobbing. After a while, she looked at me through a pair of misty eyes, "Vivian, I did not abandon Brian or his father. I never got married again, nor did I have any kids after Brian."

I was stunned. If she didn't abandon Brian, why was she missing for all those years? If she didn't remarry and have kids, who were those people in the house whom Brian saw through the window in Paris? It just didn't add up.

Michael climbed on my lap. "Grandma, so what happened?"

"Nick and I fell in love when we were in college. He—"

"Is Nick my Daddy's Poppa?"

I tried to stop Michael but it was too late.

"Michael, yes. Nick is your Grandfather, your Daddy's Poppa. Nick was an over-achiever. He came from a poor background and he vowed to conquer the world. He was very intelligent, and a linguist, so he was recognized even when we were still in school. Not long after he graduated, he was hired by the foreign service, we traveled all over the world whenever he got new assignments.

"Then we had Brian. I thought I had everything. Brian was my Little Prince. He rocked my world, and he was my world." Colleen sank into a trance again. She was humming a song. It must have been a song that she used to sing for Brian when he was little.

"Nick was appointed as an ambassador not long after we had Brian. He well deserved it, but from that point on, his work seemed to take precedence over his family. Gradually I found my husband becoming proud and arrogant. I kind of closed one eye to all the rumors, because to me as long as he loved Brian and me, the rest didn't matter. I did voice concerns about his busy late night schedule, but he would get angry and yell at me, so I kept telling myself it was a price we had to pay for success. Then the lies got exposed."

"What lies?" I sensed the inevitable.

Colleen gave me a bitter smile. "Well, since Michael is here. Let's just say I caught him cheating. Brian and I were supposed to go on a trip back to France to visit my family but due to a severe winter storm, the plane was canceled. We took a cab home.

"When the maid answered the door, her face turned white and she started to scream. I thought something was wrong with Nick, so I rushed to the second floor to check on him. Then I saw the most ugly picture in my own bedroom. I had to flee from the scene so I wouldn't throw up. He was with another woman, on our bed." Colleen closed her eyes. Her hands were shaking as she recalled that horrible sight.

"I ran down the stairs and took Brian for a long walk. I didn't tell him what I had seen, because I was in denial and in shock. Besides, Nick was his father. Brian always had great respect for his father and I was not cruel enough to break that trust."

Then she looked at me, "Vivian, do you think I did the right thing? You must think I was the most foolish woman who ever lived, but things were very different back then. We were taught to keep quiet because we women were the cause of men's unhappiness.

"Being an ambassador's wife, I had to put on a beautiful show at all times so he wouldn't lose respect from his peers or miss a promotion. People didn't care so much about what happened behind the curtains, because it was considered dirty laundry which should remain hidden at all times."

"So what happened after that?"

"I tried to stay for Brian's sake, but the word got out. It was a big scandal, because the woman involved was another ambassador's wife. I asked for a divorce after that. Nick finally consented but he wanted Brian. He told me that I only had one choice, which was to return to France or else he would make sure I never saw Brian again.

"He told me that he could easily get rid of me without anyone suspecting, and he would do it if I forced his hand. He made me sign a document saying that I would only see Brian under his supervision, and then he arranged my trip back to France with an escort.

"I had no choice. I left with a broken heart. My marriage had ended, my son was taken from me, and my world was ripped apart. The first thing I thought of was my music; at least I could find some comfort in it. I picked up where I had left off before the marriage, and buried myself in it. I was recognized in the music world, and I started performing, recording music, and teaching students. I had to find a way out of my misery and music provided that escape—"

"So what Brian saw through the window was not your new family, but your students maybe?"

She paused. "That's most likely. My students ranged from toddlers to seniors and we were close, like a family."

"What about the gentleman Brian saw next to you?"

"The only possible person I can think of is my cousin Wesley, who moved to France from Australia about the same time I moved back. Brian had never met him. Wesley came to visit my apartment often and he played better piano than I do, so I would listen to him play. He wrote his own music and he could play by ear."

I let out a long breath. Finally we were able to put the pieces together. "Did you ever visit him? Brian couldn't get over the fact that you never missed him or visited him, and he was told that you remarried."

Colleen suddenly said, "excuse me" and left the room. She returned, holding a bunch of air tickets and letters. She showed me the dates when she had flown to see Brian.

"I flew out many times to see him — every year for his birthday, graduation, until he reached fifteen, but his father prohibited me from seeing him face to face. He couldn't afford a scandal, and our divorce had cost him a big promotion. These letters were returned marked 'moved.'" Colleen shook her head.

Michael said, "Grandma, you are right. Nick is wrong."

Colleen put her hands around Michael's face and sighed, "Michael, I wish life was that simple. I should have stayed with your father regardless of the scandal. At least your Dad would not have hated me for abandoning him."

Michael held her hands, "Grandma, now you are wrong. Daddy never hated you. He told me that. He said you were a beautiful and classy lady with so much love, just like my Mama, and he said if one day I saw you, I must tell you that he loves you very much."

I was shocked when I heard Michael's words. *When did Brian talk with him about Colleen?*

Colleen cried on my shoulder. She held Michael and me tight. Then Mindy woke up. She came into the room, asking, "Is Grandma all right? Why is she crying, Mommy?"

"Baby, everything is all right. Go back to sleep." I gave her a kiss.

I turned around and saw Michael hugging his Grandma. At that brief moment, I thought Colleen was holding Brian. I stood there watching Colleen embracing Michael, and I knew she was trying to make up for all the lost time with her Little Prince.

I smiled and looked up. "Brian, do you see that?"

CHAPTER 13

After Brian turned fifteen, Colleen lost contact with Brian and his father altogether. Colleen then had to tend her sick parents until they died, and she was kept busy with concerts.

Colleen stayed another three days upon our earnest urging, but she had to perform in a concert. We saw her off at the airport. Michael and Mindy were trying their best to convince her to move back to the States after retirement. With a smile she replied, "I will seriously think about it, I promise." I told her she was welcome anytime.

I finally posed the question about Brian's eyesight. "Colleen, do you know anything about Brian's eyesight? Do you think he was born colorblind?"

"Colorblind?" Colleen wasn't sure. She looked puzzled.

I explained to her what I had been told by Dr. Field about Michael's colorblindness and Achromatopsia.

She was not certain. "Brian had poor eyesight, and his eyes were always sensitive to light, but we never took it seriously.

"Vivian, as you know, in the old days technology was not as advanced, so if people did in fact have colorblindness, more than often they just coped with it. To tell you the truth, I never heard of Achromatopsia. I don't even recall anyone that I knew of who was colorblind."

CHAPTER 14

I had avoided going home to visit Poppa and Mama after Brian's passing. Deep down I blamed Poppa for his seeming curse that 'Brian was one foot in the grave'. I knew Poppa felt sorry about his quick tongue, but I still held a grudge against him.

Poppa, Mama and everyone else kept calling and telling me that I had another home to visit, but I just kept ignoring them. At the same time, Michael and Mindy inquired often when we were going to visit their family, and I always used our busy schedule as the excuse until Mama called me out of the blue one day.

"Vivian, when are you coming home?" Mama asked.

I hesitated, but then answered in a firm voice. "Mama, my home is here with Michael and Mindy."

I heard a deep sigh from the other end of the phone. "Vivian, I don't see you any more. I don't see my grandkids any more. Your Dad and I mourned enough for losing Brian whom we took in as our own son. Now you are telling me that I also have to mourn for the loss of a daughter and two grandkids? You cannot be that cruel."

My heart pained me, but I refused to give in. I didn't answer.

Mama said, "I know you are mad at your Dad, but this cold war has lasted long enough. Yes, he had troubles accepting Brian at first, but that was because he cared about you and wanted you to have the best. After the whole family decided to accept Brian, your

Dad did too, and in fact he blamed himself for Brian's death. Vivian, how many more years do you think your Dad and I can enjoy you or our grandkids' being around? Please do not take away that pleasure due us." Mama started to choke up.

My heart melted. I gave in and assured her that we would visit her soon.

By then, I had started working for a medical billing company and was on a flexible schedule, so I told Michael and Mindy that we would visit Grandpa and Grandma for a few days. They jumped up and down out of excitement! I realized my selfishness had not only robbed Mama and Poppa of their joy, but Michael and Mindy as well.

Michael loved to wander around the fields, talking with trees, grass, flowers, dogs, cats, chickens and bugs, while Mindy liked to sing to them and paint pictures of them. On top of that, they loved to be spoiled by their grandparents, uncles, and aunts.

On the night we arrived, Michael had so much fun playing with Poppa. I enjoyed watching them laugh. Michael tried to teach Poppa to pronounce words without his southern accent, and the harder Poppa tried, the funnier his words sounded.

Poppa joked at Michael, "Michael, you do know you are teaching an old dog a new trick, right?"

Then Michael mounted on top of Poppa and directed him to move toward his left or right. Poppa spun so hard that Michael fell off. Then it was Mindy's turn. She fell too. Then Poppa tickled them until they laughed and cried for help. I realized that through the reconnection with Mama and Poppa, Michael and Mindy somehow had gained their childhood back.

I never told Poppa about Mama's call that triggered my decision to return home, but I could tell from his face that he was relieved, comforted, and delighted to see us. The first night after supper, Poppa with a beer bottle in his hand, walked up to me. He placed his hand on my shoulder and said, "Vivian, good to see you home."

I nodded. "Thank you, Poppa."

Then there was silence. I felt the evening breeze on my face. I closed my eyes welcoming the cool air.

Poppa broke the silence. "Vivian, you have mourned for a long time. It is time to reach down deep to your gut and pull the plug."

"Poppa, I am not built that way. Besides, there is no plug in place for me to pull. My pit is pretty dark down there and I see no end of it." I replied, with a bit of resentment.

He was not offended. Instead, he shook his head. "You know your old man is never good with words, and they never come out right."

I didn't say anything. I thought he was half drunk.

He became quiet for some time. Nodding his head, he then said, "You do know that if your old man could have traded places with Brian, he would have done that, right?"

"But why?" I asked.

He stared at me, and then gazed into the house where Michael and Mindy were. I had never seen Poppa this serious.

He answered, "When Brian was really sick, I asked God to take me instead, but He didn't. I still don't know why. Vivian, you will find out soon that there are two hardest things for parents to bear: one is to see their kids suffer, and the other is to bury them. And I got both." He sighed as he stood up and quietly walked away.

Does that mean Poppa loves me and Brian no less than he loves Josh, Paul, Victoria or Elizabeth?

Being the middle child and daughter, I always felt that I was skipped over. No one really paid attention to me, unless they needed meals prepared, clothes ironed, or errands run. Everything I got was leftover from my two older brothers and two younger sisters, including love and attention.

But Poppa was willing to trade places with Brian because he did love Brian and wanted to spare me pain and heartache. *Does that mean he loves me too?* I felt validated that night.

CHAPTER 15

Then one night Ruth returned. She stood in front of Poppa's house knocking, but no one heard her. Michael happened to look out of the window, and saw her standing there like a ghost. Michael had never met Ruth before, so he called Poppa to answer the door. I was helping Mama in the kitchen with dishes. Suddenly I heard Poppa yelling from the living room.

"Who are you? No solicitations here." Then he recognized her. "How dare you show up at my door? Leave my son and my grandchildren alone. You've hurt them enough."

Mama and I ran to the door and saw Ruth begging to come in. I almost could not recognize her. She had lost a lot of weight, and her face and body were all bruised. The Ruth I remembered was totally different from the one standing before me.

Ruth used to have a round face with a little baby fat, but it was all gone. She looked at least fifty, yet she was only in her early thirties. Even her voice sounded different. She used to have a childlike sweet voice, but now it was low and husky.

What had happened to her? I remembered her pure innocent personality, contagious laughter, and her crafty hands. Ruth loved kids and worked as a teacher at the same school with Paul, that's where they had met and fallen in love. They were so much in love. *How did they fall out of love?*

Mama and I finally were able to convince Poppa to let Ruth in. Michael was startled by Ruth's appearance. Ruth had never met Michael before, so I could see confusion in her eyes, but somehow Michael triggered something in her so that she started to cry. Then I realized Michael must have reminded Ruth of her own kids, Meagan and Jay.

Seeing Ruth's tears streaming down, Poppa didn't know what to do so he paced back and forth in the room. Mama went to the kitchen to fix some tea. I talked to Ruth. "Ruth, you have missed out so much. While you were away, I got married and had two kids. Michael is five and Mindy is four. Time just flew by." I put my hand on her shoulder.

Ruth finally was able to look at me. "Vivian, it is so kind of you to talk to me. Bless your heart." Then she started sobbing again.

Mama came back with a cup of tea. It was her soothing remedy and it worked every time. We saw Ruth gradually stop crying.

"Poppa and Mama, please forgive me. I came back to beg for forgiveness. Vivian, please forgive me. I committed the greatest sin and I know Paul will never forgive me, but I have to confess to him and to Meagan and Jay or I will never have peace.

"Paul can divorce me, report me for adultery, put me in prison, or even kill me. I don't care, but please allow me to see him and the kids. Please…I beg you, Poppa." Ruth's eyes were all swollen and her tears smeared her face.

We sat there for almost five minutes without a word, not because we didn't have comments to make, but because we didn't know where to start. Finally Mama let out a long sigh, a thin one, yet it spoke all our disappointments. Then Poppa sighed.

I heard Michael sigh as well, and I turned to him, signaling him not to interfere in the adults' business, but his little face had a look of an old sage, with his eyes staring at an unknown space.

I said, "Ruth, I think you know why Poppa and Mama are so mad at you. You crushed Paul when you packed and left. You took every ounce of life out of him. He cannot handle another betrayal."

Ruth looked me in the eyes, "Vivian, I want to face up to everyone in the family, especially Paul. I want to confess my wrongs before him and the kids, and then I will leave, I promise, and I will never bother any of you again. Please grant me your mercy."

How is Paul going to react to all this? What about Meagan and Jay?

After seeing Ruth's genuine outpouring of her regret, Poppa and Mama's hearts softened. I suggested Ruth come back the next day. She looked even more distraught. Lowering her head, she mumbled, "I have no place to go."

Feeling sorry for her, and sensing she was on the brink of collapse, I then took the liberty to ask her to stay at the house for the night. Poppa gave me a harsh glance. He wanted to say something but Mama stopped him before he opened his mouth, so he made a weird grumbling sound from his deep throat.

"Are you turning into a wolf?" Mama asked him. Mama told Ruth she could stay in Victoria's old bedroom. After Ruth retreated to her room, Poppa, Mama and I sat around the table. Mama fixed more tea.

Poppa cleared his throat. "I don't think this is a good idea. Paul was like a zombie for several years. He finally got hold of himself. I am afraid he will lose it again if they see each other."

Mama looked over at Poppa, "Paul is an adult. He should be the one to decide if they should meet. It is between them. Besides, Meagan is going to be a teenager and desperately needs a mother to guide her. Jay needs a mother to nurture him as well."

Surprisingly, Poppa and Mama turned to me, "Vivian, what do you think?"

I paused. Then I spoke very slowly, "I don't know whether Paul can forgive her or not." Then I noticed someone pulling my shirt. I looked down. It was Michael. He stood between Mama and me.

"Grandpa, Grandma, and Mommy, Jesus forgave a woman who did a very bad thing, too. It is in the Bible." Michael looked at us in a serious manner.

"Michael has been reading the Bible." I said to Poppa and Mama. "We all know an old saying: once a mirror is broken, it is hard to glue it back."

Michael pulled my shirt again, "Jesus is the super glue. He can do it."

Poppa and Mama looked at Michael, then looked at me in disbelief. Poppa touched Michael's head, "Hey, kid, do you really know what you are talking about? I wish it was that simple." He then sat back on his couch, grabbed the remote control and resumed his normal position in front of the TV, which was his way of escaping.

Mama had a doubting look for some time. Then she looked at Michael and smiled, "Michael, I thought you were only five years old but you sounded fifty. You are a smart cookie all right. Do you want some real cookies? I've saved some special ones for you."

Michael's eyes popped. He followed Mama to the kitchen.

Meanwhile I felt the need to talk with Ruth to clarify something that had bothered me for a long while.

Her door was open. Ruth was sitting at the edge of the bed glaring at the window. I made some noise before walking in, and she immediately turned around. When she saw me, her eyes lit up.

"Vivian, did you say your boy's name is Michael? He has your cheekbones and lips. He is a handsome boy. You said you had two kiddos? What's the other one's name?" Ruth always loved kids, that's why it was so mindboggling that she would have left her own.

I sat on the chair across from her. "Yup! Michael is his name all right. Thank you for the compliment. The other one is a girl, and her name is Mindy. In fact, Mindy is playing with Meagan right now as we speak. They are at Liz's place."

When Meagan's name was brought up, Ruth's eyes turned red. She grabbed my hands and asked, "How is Meagan? How is Jay doing? Are they all right?"

I touched her hands and noticed they were just skin and bones. "What happened to you, Ruth? You don't look all right. Are you ill?" I couldn't imagine what she had gone through to become like this.

"Vivian, it is my punishment. I don't blame anyone but myself. That's why I came back. I don't expect you, Paul, or anyone to forgive me, but I have to let everyone know that I am sorry for what I have done and put you through."

Ruth cried as she finished her sentence. She paused to breathe through her mouth and continued, "Vivian, I grew up in a dirt poor family and have always wanted 'good' stuff. After marrying Paul, I was never satisfied, and I complained to him all the time about our lack of money.

"One day at school, a man came up to me, thanking me for my patience and care for his child. He said his wife had passed away, so his son needed additional attention. He also complimented me on my beauty. I had never gotten that kind of affirmation from Paul or anyone, so right away his words grabbed my heart. See how naive I was!"

Ruth shook her head with a bitter smile before she continued. "Afterward he came by almost every other day. At first he asked me for coffee, and then lunch, and then dinner. He would buy me flowers, jewelry, or anything I mentioned to him that I was lacking. Then we had an affair." Ruth shook her head. She closed her eyes.

My stomach turned upside down. *What about my poor brother Paul?*

"I told Paul many lies during that time, and those lies finally caught up to me. Paul noticed my attitude toward him and the kids had changed, so one day he asked for the truth. I knew I couldn't lie any more so I spilled it out. He was shocked, but asked me not to leave for the kids' sake. He never once said he needed me or loved me, so I used that as an excuse to continue seeing that guy behind Paul's back, until one day Paul caught us together after school.

"He was furious and he knocked that guy down, and then he left without saying a word to me. I thought he was too mad to be rational so I sneaked into the house, packed my stuff, and then left to be with that guy." Ruth looked at the bed sheet.

"Vivian, I was wrong. I had it all wrong. That man's wife hadn't died, as he told me. She was abused, fearing for her life, and she fled out of state. You see, a lie for a lie. I lied to Paul and I was lied to. After I went to be with him, he pretended to be Prince Charming for a few months. He first cheated on me with some other girls at his office. When I got jealous, he laughed at me, scorned me, and called me 'whore.'"

I shivered, wanting to block my ears. Ruth immediately apologized, "I am sorry, I shouldn't have said that word. Vivian. He then started beating me. I threatened to leave him and report him, and the beatings got worse. He told me no one on earth would pity me, believe me or help me. He said I was an adulterous wife and an unfit mother. I was useless and my family would never forgive me. One day he kicked me, and threatened to kill me and my kids if I ever left." Ruth suddenly lost it and collapsed in bed.

I was partially numb. These were the things you saw on TV or read in the newspaper. They were not supposed to happen in real life, at least not in my family. "Ruth, let's talk about this tomorrow. You are too tired."

"Vivian, I am so sorry—please let me say I'm sorry to Paul, Meagan, and Jay. I beg you…" Ruth whispered as she gradually fell into sleep.

I walked out of her room, exhausted. *Is Paul capable of forgiving her?* Paul had tried so hard to shut off his past so he could live his present. Before Ruth's departure, he had been optimistic about life and people. After she left, he aged twenty years overnight, and became extremely quiet. The first few years he hid himself from the rest of the family, and then he had come back, still acting like a stranger. Gradually he got better, and during the last year and a half he had found peace through a church and started serving in the community. I never visited his church and wasn't sure what he did there, but I was told that he had helped out many single parents.

Paul told me once that his 'burden' was to help others who shared a similar pain. *What kind of burden was that?* It didn't make sense to me.

I walked out of Ruth's room and told Mama and Michael that I needed to visit Paul. Poppa had already fallen asleep in front of the TV with the remote control in his hand. Mama first hesitated, but consented. Michael didn't say anything, but gave me a hug. Paul was Michael's favorite uncle and they shared the same hobby — fishing.

I told Michael not to wait for me to go to bed. "I will pick up Mindy. Michael, make sure you take off your socks and take a bath before going to bed. Grandma will help you if Mommy gets home late. Kiss Mommy good night."

Michael gave me a kiss, whispering in my ear, "Mommy, I love you. Can you tell Uncle Paul that Jesus saves and Jesus also forgives?"

I kissed him back, "I love you too. I will tell him, but don't wait up."

CHAPTER 16

It took me about twenty minutes to stroll to Paul's house. As I expected he was still up working on a school project.

"Vivian, what brings you here? I heard from Liz that you and the kids were in town." He was holding a binder as he greeted me.

I glanced through the house, wondering why Paul had gotten this sloppy. No wonder Liz always took Meagan and Jay to her house.

Paul apologized for the mess, but I could see he didn't really know how to take care of himself, so how could I expect him to take care of the house or the kids?

I sat down and found a shirt underneath me, so I picked it up, folded it and placed it on the table. "Paul, how are you doing? I haven't really talked to you since Brian passed away. I didn't know what to say, or should I say we were both busy mourning for our loss? Remember when we were little, we were buddies? Since when have we become strangers?"

"Vivian, you want some tea?"

"Let me do it." I walked into the kitchen to fix myself tea and offered him a cup. He declined first, but accepted it as I insisted. As I was trying to find the mugs, I started cleaning his kitchen. Dirty dishes filled the sink, so I washed them and put them away. Paul walked in, and offered to help.

"Paul, do you still love Ruth?"

He almost dropped a dish. Paul was known for his introvert qualities. It would take an act of God for him to open up, but I had to give it a try. I had to see whether his broken heart could ever be mended.

"Sis, why do you ask? It is no use to talk about it now," said Paul.

"What if there is a chance for you and Ruth to get back together?"

"Vivian, what brings this up? Is this what you want to talk about tonight?"

I turned around to start the dishwasher and started picking up his clothes on the floor. They needed to be washed and ironed. "Paul, before I came, Michael asked me to tell you something. I didn't quite get it but he thought you would."

Paul's face lit up. I knew Michael had a special place in his heart. They clicked.

"What did Michael say? He is such a special kid. Vivian, you are very blessed to have him."

"He said Jesus saves and Jesus forgives. He also said Jesus is the glue for all broken relationships. These are his words. What do you think? Can Jesus really help? I thought once a mirror is broken, it could never be whole again, but obviously Michael thought otherwise, and he asked me to tell you that."

Paul sat down. Then he looked me straight in the eyes, "Did Ruth come back? Is she here?"

"Ruth came to Poppa's house. Yes, she is there. She wanted to see you and the kids and apologized for what she had done to you. Paul, she looked horrible. She was abused and her body was broken. I talked to her and

True Rainbow

she told me everything. She begged Poppa, Mama and me to allow her to see you and the kids." I stopped to see Paul's reaction.

The muscle right below his right eye twitched. I saw hurt and sorrow. He looked like a statue.

"She didn't expect you to forgive her, but begged you to give her a chance to confess."

Paul closed his eyes. I was afraid that he was about to shut me out as he had a few years ago. "Paul, I don't mean to interfere in your affairs, but after Brian died, I wished that I could turn back the clock. If so, I would hold Brian tight every day, tell him I love him every hour, and treasure every moment we spent together. I guess that's why I asked you whether you still love Ruth. If the answer is yes, and if you can forgive her, please don't let this opportunity slip by."

Paul turned his back to pick up something from the floor. I knew he needed some time alone, so I came near him and hugged him from behind. "Paul, you are my brother, and I will always support your decision. We all will."

Then I left. I went by Liz's house to pick up Mindy and to see Meagan and Jay. When I got there, they were playing hide-and-seek with Elizabeth's two boys, Luke and Johnny.

I told Liz about Ruth's return. She was stunned by the news and said, "I know what Victoria will say if she learns about this."

"What will she say?"

"She will tell Ruth to take a hike and get out of Poppa's house immediately. She will chase her out. Victoria has no sympathy for Ruth."

Liz was right about Victoria. *But is Victoria wrong? Does she act out our anger so we can all hide underneath the blanket of pretentious kindness?*

If I could react to my first instincts, I would scream at Ruth for what she had done to Paul, Meagan, Jay and the whole family. I would shake her and then block my ears from all her apologies. She betrayed and violated my brother's trust, her own children's, and the whole family's. *How could she do such a thing to those who love her?*

I am a hypocrite! I suddenly realized my own fallacy. *Is Ruth really on the stand waiting for the sentence? Who is the judge? Am I the judge? Is Victoria the judge? Who gives us the right to judge Ruth? Are we really better than she is?*

Michael's words came to me, "could you tell Uncle Paul that Jesus saves and Jesus forgives?" Then Pastor Franklin's sermon flooded in. "You and I are not perfect either, so we are looking at a world that is imperfect because it is made of imperfect people like you and me, and the truth is that we are part of the problem, not the solution. We've all sinned. Sin is anything that we might have offended God with, such as our imperfect thoughts or deeds. Since God is perfect and holy, anything imperfect or unholy offends Him. It maybe our lying tongue, our impure and selfish motives, covetousness, lustful thoughts or simply nodding your head to the least of harm or shutting your eyes to the least of good…"

Suddenly my palms began to sweat and my heart began pounding. *Does that mean I am also a sinner like Ruth in God's eyes?*

"What are you thinking?"

I quickly shook my head, "Nothing," and threw the question back at her, "Liz, what do you think? Yes, Ruth did something wrong, but haven't we all?"

She thought for a while, and then answered me, "You are asking the wrong person. You and I are not the prime victims in this scenario. Paul and the kids are. He is our brother and I've witnessed what he's gone through, and the kids. Vivian, you don't live here but I do. For you, it is out of sight, out of mind, but I didn't have that luxury. The heartache almost ate Paul alive. The kids were lost; they felt shame but dared not ask questions about their mother.

"They used to be loved by everyone but suddenly they were pushed down and trampled on the ground by their neighbors and scoffed at by their schoolmates. Did you notice smiles disappeared from their little faces for a long time? That's why I took them in. I just couldn't bear to see them suffer like that.

"I don't know the answer but I know one thing: forgiveness should be given if there is true repentance. I just don't know whether Ruth has come to that true repentance. Does she deserve our forgiveness, or is this just her way to save herself?"

"Liz, my question to you and all of us is, who is the judge of Ruth's true repentance? You and I cannot serve as judges, because neither one of us sees her heart. So how can we judge her about her repentance? Do we punish her for what she has put us through and call it justice?

"Does shutting her out really offer the best prospect for Paul and the kids? Yes, I have not been the witness to their pain and shame as you have, but I am also their aunt, and I want the best for them. The bottom line is, Ruth is not perfect, neither are you and I. We all need forgiveness somewhere and sometime in life."

Liz looked straight at me and replied, "If I were Paul, I wouldn't take her back."

I said, "I just hope that I won't do anything to get on your bad side, or else I am forever doomed."

Liz laughed. "You'd better not."

We both laughed. Mindy and Meagan came up to me, asking me to join their hide-and-seek game, so I gladly obliged. It was indeed a lot of fun to be the oldest in the bunch because I had to play the clown. It had always been Brian's job, but now it fell on me. We laughed and laughed.

Finally Mindy and I were ready to leave. She fell asleep on my shoulder. Liz walked us to the door and we gave each other a kiss on the cheek. I asked her another question. "What if you were Ruth? Don't you want to make things right?"

"Viv, if I were her, I would not have made that stupid mistake to begin with. What was she thinking to walk out of the family and leave her husband and kids behind? I would rather kill myself than show up demanding forgiveness."

"She didn't demand it. She is begging for it. Liz, you should see her. She is no longer the Ruth we knew. She has lost everything: her beauty, her confidence, her self-esteem, and probably her hope for the future."

"Isn't that called justice well served? Viv, let's not fight over this. I am not ready to forgive her just yet. Deep down I am still resentful for what she had put Paul, the kids, and all of us through."

I nodded. "I am not trying to convince you, but I do want to ask for a favor…If you cannot be supportive, please at least be neutral if Paul decides to forgive her."

"I will think about it." We gave each other a hug, and Liz gave Mindy a kiss before we headed for the street.

Feeling the kiss, Mindy woke up. As we walked down the road, Mindy started murmuring to me about how much fun she had with her cousins. "Mommy, I like Jay. He likes me too."

"Do you like Luke and Johnny? They are your cousins and they are very nice too."

"Mommy, they are old." Mindy gave me a serious look, as if I was making a big mistake.

"Excuse me. Your Dad was old, but you used to want to marry him?"

Mindy didn't even think before she replied. "Mommy, that's different. Daddy is Daddy and he is special."

"But why do you like Jay that much?"

"Mommy, you know Jay doesn't have a mother? He sometimes cries and hides from everyone, but he told me he liked me so he won't hide from me. Mommy, do you think we can find Jay a Mommy?"

I heard a sigh from my heart. *Children's hearts are so tender and soft because they have not been contaminated by this world or hardened by hate and betrayal. They don't have a problem with forgiveness. Is God's heart also tender and soft? Is it how God can forgive sin?*

We arrived at Poppa's house. Poppa was in his same position, still holding the remote control and snoring away. Mama had already gone to bed. I put Mindy down on the sofa first, and woke up Poppa, trying to assist him to his room.

Poppa opened one eye to look at me. "Don't mind me. You need to go to bed." He managed to grope his way back to his room, with his eyes shut.

Michael was reading a book when Mindy and I entered the room. He was too focused to notice our presence. He was just like his Dad, a typical night owl.

"Michael, what did I say earlier? Don't wait up but go to bed."

"I tried, but I wanted to wait for you and Mindy."

I gave in. After everyone was clean, teeth brushed, and changed to their pajamas, Michael and Mindy climbed into bed and took their sides, Michael on my right and Mindy on the left. I closed my eyes, but my mind was racing. One minute I saw Brian walking behind me asking me to wait for him, and the next minute I saw Paul's face.

Then Michael pulled on my pajamas, so I placed my hand on his back, "Michael, can't sleep?"

"Mommy, so what did Uncle Paul say?" He lowered his voice so we wouldn't wake up Mindy.

"Uncle Paul didn't say anything. You know he needed some time to think things through, but he is a grown-up and he can take care of himself, so don't worry about it. You need to go to sleep in order to grow taller and stronger."

Then I heard nothing for a while, but somehow by his breathing I knew he was still awake.

"Michael, are you still up?" I asked.

"Yes, Mommy. I am praying for Uncle Paul, Aunt Ruth, Meagan, and Jay." He replied.

CHAPTER 17

It was not even seven o'clock. Mama was cooking breakfast, while Poppa enjoyed his morning ritual—reading the newspaper—and the rest of us sat around the kitchen table waking up as we were waiting to be fed. Ruth was still in her room and we decided to wake her up later.

Then we heard a knock on the door, followed by Meagan's voice, saying "Grandpa, Grandma, we are here!"

Without thinking, with the frying pan in her hand, Mama rushed out to open the door. Jay and Meagan followed Mama to the kitchen and they sat down next to us. They both looked starved, so I offered them toast and grits.

"Aunt Vivian, can I have oatmeal and eggs? Jay would like an omelet with a lot of ham."

Jay said, "no, I don't want an omelet, I want a peanut butter sandwich."

"No, Mommy said peanut butter was not for breakfast. You need protein!"

I stopped the argument by placing them on different sides of the table, "I will give Jay an omelet and a peanut butter sandwich. How about that? By the way, Meagan, don't you want to talk to Mindy?"

Then Paul walked in. He wore a newly washed and ironed shirt, and he had combed his hair. Michael jumped from his chair and went to give Paul a warm hug. Paul put Michael on his lap and gave me a wry smile. "Vivian, do you think I can ask for some breakfast as well?"

Mama resumed her cooking. She asked me, "Vivian, do you want to wake up Ruth so she can have breakfast with us?"

I nodded and headed toward Ruth's room.

Paul stopped me, "Vivian, I think I should be the one to wake her up, if you won't mind?"

"Certainly not!"

Then we heard knocks on the door again. Mama murmured, "What's going on? Did we invite all the neighbors for breakfast? Poppa, did you send out an invitation?"

Poppa was still reading his newspaper. "Uh…"

It was Victoria and Elizabeth. They walked into the kitchen, and Victoria's high-pitched voice woke everyone up.

"Mama, we followed the aroma of your cooking. When I learned through the grapevine that we are going to have a summit meeting, I didn't even have a chance to put my make-up on." Victoria placed her hands on my shoulders, implying that I was the one who tipped off the secret.

I passed Liz a look. She said with a smile, "Vivian, I thought we joined you for breakfast this morning. We rarely do this kind of family gatherings since you left the family for college."

"So where is everybody?" Victoria asked.

"What do you mean? We are all here." I knew what she meant, but decided to play along.

Liz touched my elbow. "Where is Ruth?"

Victoria said, "You know, the tradition still holds true in terms of passing votes in this household, right, Poppa?" Poppa's attention was still focused on the "Dear Abby" column so he declined to answer, until Victoria repeated the question.

"What? Emergency? You think I am deaf? Well, I am half deaf, but still, you don't need to be that loud."

I said, "Poppa, don't you agree that the matter between Paul and Ruth should be resolved by them and no one else?"

Poppa looked at me, at Liz, and at Victoria. "Any one wants to challenge it? It is between them and the kids."

Victoria wouldn't give up. "So what's the purpose of our family tradition, then? Poppa, you were the one that made the rules, if my memory serves me right. I was four when you taught us the democratic system in this household. That shows we care because we are one family. Since when have you decided to abolish the system?"

Suddenly, I heard Paul's voice from the background, "Victoria, this time is different."

"What's the difference? I don't see any." Victoria rolled her eyes.

Paul walked closer, stood in front of her, and replied, "The difference between now and then is this: The voting system took place when we were young, because back then we were not mature enough to make decisions of our own so we needed the family's counsel, whereas now we are old enough to decide what would be best for our own families.

"If you really want to show me you sincerely care about me, then let me make my own decision, and support it. Show your true care by showing me your respect of my decision, Sis."

Victoria simmered with rage. "Well, if you don't want my input, don't blame me when that woman leaves you again for another man."

Paul's face got bright red, but then he calmed down, "I never blamed anyone. Yes, I am thankful for what you, Liz, and everyone has done for Meagan and Jay, which I can never repay. However, I cannot blame Ruth either. I wasn't a good enough husband. I didn't make her feel that I loved her enough.

"Sis, We all fall short, you and I both. No human is perfect. Neither you nor I dare claim the righteousness to cast the first stone. Do you know two thousand years ago Jesus, being the perfect Man, never condemned but forgave the sinning woman? So, case closed!" Paul went toward the bedroom.

Poppa dropped his newspaper and looked at us three girls, "That's my boy. What can I say?"

Where did that come from? Mama must have had a heart-to-heart talk with Poppa last night to convince him to stay out of Paul's family business.

Meantime, Mama urged everyone to eat breakfast.

Michael sat on his chair observing the whole proceeding without saying a word. His eyes revealed a gleam of hope and his nod of approval reminded me of an old sage. He noticed my looking at him so he gave me a smile and two thumbs up.

Mindy was playing with Meagan with her dolls from Colleen. They were in their own small world. I was thankful that their hearts were not stirred by the adult conversation.

Victoria finally sat down with Liz. Mama fixed them toast and eggs. Feeling awkward, I tried to come up with some topics to change the conversation. "Hey, I heard the city is thinking of expanding the Public Library. Wouldn't that be great for the locals."

Victoria ignored me. Liz turned to me. "They already planned a groundbreaking ceremony to kick off the major construction. Where did you get your news?"

Victoria said, "Probably from Poppa's old newspaper. Hey, Poppa, when are you going to get rid of all your expired newspapers? Since the library has more room now, why don't you donate your old newspapers to them?"

We all agreed it was a great idea, yet Poppa yelled, "No one touches my papers!" His face turned red.

Then we all burst into laughter.

Paul came in with Ruth. I couldn't believe she was the same Ruth I had seen the night before. She was still pale, with the same clothes on, and the same bruises on her face; in fact, the bruises looked more distinct in the daylight. However, her eyes were glowing, her lips curved upward, and her manner was peaceful.

Out of the corner of my eye I saw Victoria and Liz were taken aback by Ruth's appearance, just as I had been. They were speechless for some time until Meagan ran across us to greet her mother.

Meagan got hold of Ruth's waist and threw herself on her, screaming "Mommy, Mommy. I missed you so much. Are you coming back this time forever?"

Ruth knelt down to hug Meagan. They embraced each other so tightly that no power on earth could separate them. I turned around to see where Jay was, since he hadn't come forward. He was sitting in the back with an estranged look. *It is not possible that he forgot about his own mother.* His response troubled me.

Paul beckoned Jay to come to his mother.

"No! She is not my mother. She left us. I don't know her," Jay yelled, and bolted from the house.

Paul ran after him. I wanted to go after them but Liz stopped me. "Remember, this is Paul's family affair. Didn't you just say we shouldn't interfere? Jay needs some time to digest the whole thing."

Ruth finally let go of Meagan, but witnessed the response of her own son. She was greatly saddened by that. Tears streamed down her face and she turned aside to wipe them. She recognized the damage she had done.

Liz sighed and then turned to Ruth, "I am not going to lie to you. It has been extremely hard for Jay. It is going to take him a while to look at you or call you mother."

Victoria walked up to Ruth. I knew she wanted to spill out her rage on behalf of Paul and the kids, but as soon as she eyed Meagan who was standing in front of Ruth protecting her mother, Victoria swallowed back her anger.

Poppa cleared his throat. "Ruth, ever since the moment you married Paul, you have been like a daughter to us. Children make mistakes, but we also have to teach all of you how to face up to your wrongs and the consequences. You are a teacher, and you know better than I about disciplines. I only want to say one thing to conclude this final meeting." Then Poppa stopped.

Then Poppa smiled, "Welcome back! Ruth. Welcome home!"

Ruth lowered her head and hugged Meagan. Tears flooded all over her again. Then I heard Ruth praise God as she hugged Meagan.

Victoria was still tense. I went over and placed my hand on her shoulder, and she relaxed a bit. Then Liz also came to Victoria. I saw Mama picking up tissues to wipe away tears.

At that moment, I felt a surge of warmth. It set me pondering. *Yes, this is my home, which I tried so hard to run away from and yet am now yearning to return to, after a long tiresome journey.*

Mindy didn't want to be left out, so she ran to me. I looked for Michael.

He was standing right next to his grandpa whispering into Poppa's ear. Then they gave each other a loud high five.

Michael later told me what he said to Poppa.

"Great job! Grandpa. I am proud of you. Jesus is proud of you!"

CHAPTER 18

We succumbed to the family's urging and stayed two more days. Finally we were able to board an evening flight to LAX. By the time we arrived home, it was already past midnight.

Michael and Mindy tried to be real troopers by staying up as late as possible, but as the night fell they both were under the spell of the sleepy bug. I managed to drag them home via public transportation.

As soon as we entered the house, all of us collapsed on the sofa. Suddenly I noticed the bright red voicemail blinker. I forced myself up to listen to them.

There were eight messages. The first was from Pat Carey, a neighbor whose son was in Michael's class. "Vivian, you won't believe this! Little Tommy's dad left his wife and kids for some young girl, just like that, out of the blue. Everyone is talking about this. They remember what Michael had said in the class a few months ago."

The second message was from Michael's teacher, Mrs. Ross. "Mrs. Thompson, I am so sorry to bother you, but could you please give me a call when you return? This is pertaining to Tom. Well, we can talk further when you call."

The third and the fourth messages both came from another teacher who adored Michael. She too, referred to Tom's father "abandoning" his family. The fifth and sixth messages were from other parents about the same subject.

My brain started racing. *Are they calling me to tell me Michael was right? Michael was simply acting out of his anger. He didn't mean harm to Tom or Tom's father. Michael was not serious when he said those unkind words.*

But was Michael serious? Did he see things before they happened? Come on, Vivian, you are being ridiculous. That is just not possible. Michael doesn't have any magic power to tell the future and if he does, Brian and I would have been the first ones to know.

I laughed at myself and arrived at the conclusion it was nothing but a coincidence. Turning around, I saw Michael lying on the sofa with an innocent and peaceful look.

I smiled. *Michael is just a child, not some kind of Prophet.*

Then I heard a different message.

"Mrs. Thompson, how are you? This is Dr. Field, by the way. How is Michael? I want to let you know that we have treatment options that will enhance Michael's eyesight and help reduce his sensitivity to daylight. Please feel free to contact me anytime.

"Mrs. Thompson, I am wondering if you can spare some time for a cup of coffee. I would like to talk to you more about what happened to Professor Thompson and ask whether you need any help. Do feel free to call me anytime."

I was dumbfounded. *Is Dr. Field asking me out?* I shrugged off the ridiculous idea.

The last message was from Mama, who wanted to make sure we made it home. I looked at my watch, 1:55. I decided to call Mama later.

CHAPTER 19

My plan of sleeping till dawn failed miserably. About 3:30 a.m., I was woken up by Mindy's scream. I rushed over to see her sound asleep so I sat down next to her. I touched her and found her forehead covered in sweat. Then I felt someone next to me. It was Michael. He tiptoed to my side so he wouldn't wake up his sister.

"Mindy is all right. She doesn't have fever. She probably just had a bad dream. Michael, it's okay. Go back to your room."

Michael nodded, gave me a hug, and said, "Mommy, don't you think many things came together after we prayed to Jesus?"

"Michael, do you really believe in Jesus? I can tell you like that pastor a lot."

Michael nodded again. "Mommy, Jesus talks to me all the time. Oh, I like Pastor Franklin a lot. He reminds me of Daddy."

I couldn't see any similarities between Brian and Pastor Franklin, except their slim and tall body frames. *Could it be that because Michael only sees black and white, he tends to focus more on body frames?*

"Several people have called to tell Mommy about Tom's father who left his family."

Michael looked serious. "Mommy, it is not a coincidence. It is going to get worse before it gets better."

"How can it get any worse?"

"Tom's mother is going to be in a car accident and lose the baby. She is pregnant." Michael's face was downcast.

A baby? Tom's mother is pregnant? She doesn't appear to be pregnant. She's already had three kids and she told people that they couldn't afford any more children.

Shaking my head, I turned Michael toward me and looked straight into his eyes, "Michael, spreading rumors about Tom's father was already not kind. Let's forget about what you just said."

Michael gazed right at me as he replied, "Mommy, I am serious, and I am not making this up. It is going to happen today at 9:25."

"You mean this morning at 9:25?" It was almost four in the morning.

Michael nodded. His eyes looked sad.

I didn't know how to take it in. *This cannot be true. Michael cannot know these things in advance.* Then I remembered our conversation a few months ago. *Does that mean Michael sees things coming before they actually happen?*

"Michael, I remember our last conversation about this same thing. How did you learn about these things? Who told you?"

Michael pointed toward heaven. His eyes didn't blink.

"How did God tell you these things? Since when has God revealed these things to you? How come you've never told me?"

Michael hugged me around my neck and gave me a comforting smile. "Mommy, God would tell me things whenever and however He liked it. His Word would just flush out of my heart like a faucet being turned on..."

"Did you hear Him speaking?"

"Not through my ears, but through my heart. His message would flow out freely, sometimes as loud as roaring water, while other times as soft as a whisper. I heard Him as if He was right in front of me, and we sometime carried on conversations."

My jaw must have dropped. "Michael, how long have you had these experiences?" I knew my son was not crazy, but was I crazy then?

"Mommy, I know this is mind-boggling but this is real. God has talked to me since I was little. After Pastor Franklin prayed over me, God's voice became even stronger and His message clearer."

So this has something to do with the pastor? Did he cast any spells on Michael?

Then I saw Michael shaking his head in response to my thought, "Nope! Pastor Franklin does not know about this. He simply prayed for us on that Sunday. God reveals whatever He wants to reveal, whenever He wants to and however He wants to."

"Did you tell your Daddy about this?"

Michael nodded.

Then it came to me that Brian might have known about his own death before it actually took place, if Brian had inquired of Michael.

Michael nodded again. "Yes, Mommy, Daddy knew. But Daddy asked me not to tell you. He said you would be...broken." Then his face lost his glow.

My heart sank. Brian knew about it but he didn't say anything? *O Brian, how could you not tell me?*

"Mommy, please don't be mad at Daddy. He didn't say anything, because he really loved you."

I tried to shake off my resentment by asking Michael another question, "Did God tell you everything?"

This time Michael shook his head. "God has authority to withhold any information from anyone if He chooses to."

Those are big words. I suddenly realized my little boy was not as little as I thought.

Oh, what about Tom's Mom? If Michael's words were true, she is going to be hit by a car and lose her baby! I need to do something to prevent it from happening. I cannot just sit idle and do nothing.

Michael shook his head slowly in response to my thought. "Mommy, I don't think we can stop God's clock from ticking, or block God's plan from happening, because God is the One who owns and runs the universe. Time and space belong to Him."

"I know, Michael. I know. But I have to give it a try. Even though I don't know Tom's mom that well, I have to try. She just lost her husband, and she has three young kids to take care of plus one on the way. Oh my goodness. This is terrible." I started to pace back and forth.

"But, Mommy, God has a purpose for everything He does. He has His good reasons. If we try to intervene, we will only make things worse."

Ignoring Michael, I murmured to myself, "I have to do something about this. If I don't, I will regret it for the rest of my life."

It was 4:50. I still had a chance to stop the accident from taking place. Looking back at Michael and ignoring his pleading eyes, I pulled him into my arms. "Michael, I am so sorry that I didn't believe you before. This is beyond me. No matter what, God has given you this special ability. Obviously He has a special purpose for you and your life. Everything will be okay."

We hugged each other for a long time.

CHAPTER 20

I had a mission to accomplish that morning. I felt like Superwoman, who was called to save a mother and her unborn child, *but how?*

Even though I trusted Michael, I was still not one hundred percent convinced of my son's prophetic power. Yet I couldn't afford to take a chance on two lives, so I figured as long as I found a way to detain Tom's mom past 9:25 a.m., my mission would have been accomplished.

After driving Michael and Mindy to school, I drove over to a shopping center nearby. Sitting in my car, I debated what excuse I should use to keep Tom's mom until 9:25? The problem was she didn't really know me.

My watch said 8:20. I was pressed for time to find Tom's mom. So I called Pat, the neighbor who had left the first message on the voice mail, hoping that through her I could obtain Tom's home address or phone number. Pat didn't answer the phone.

I had one hour to figure that out, or else I would not be able to live with myself, so I dialed Michael's teacher, Mrs. Ross's cell number, realizing that she might not pick up the phone since school was in session. Surprisingly she answered.

"This is Eileen Ross. Who is calling?" Her voice sounded upbeat.

My tongue froze for a moment. Then I responded, "Mrs. Ross, hi. This is Michael's mom, Vivian."

"Oh, Mrs. Thompson, I am so glad that you called. I am on my way to the class. Do you mind my calling you later? We have to talk."

"Yes, no problem. But, Mrs. Ross, do you happen to have Tom's mom's phone number or their address?" I tried very hard not to reveal the urgency.

Mrs. Ross got quiet. She probably was trying to figure out my motive. "Mrs. Thompson, you do know about Tom's family situation, right?" She sounded reluctant.

I could understand her hesitancy. She probably thought I was going to give Tom's mom a hard time. "Mrs. Ross, I mean no ill will. I just want to offer her some comfort, and we plan to invite Tom and his mom over." Biting my tongue, I felt myself blushing at my lying to Mrs. Ross.

"That is very kind of you, but I can't release that information. I would get into big trouble with her and with school. I am sorry."

"Mrs. Ross, please help me. This is urgent. I have to get to her before it is too late."

Then there was silence on the other side.

"Mrs. Ross, please allow me to explain this later, but I really need to get to her in time."

Mrs. Ross was quiet for a few seconds and then answered, "Mrs. Thompson, I am so sorry to turn you down. It is a rule that I cannot break. But I can inform you that Tom's mom just dropped Tom off, and she is leaving as we speak."

"Mrs. Ross, I will call you back as soon as possible. Thank you for your help."

I immediately drove toward Michael's school. As I drove in, I passed Tom's mom, so I quickly turned around to follow her.

Tom's mom wasn't a good driver, to say the least. She beat the light, didn't stop at the stop sign, and made sudden and wide turns, which made me worry that we both might get into an accident.

I looked at my watch; it was 8:35. There was no sign that she was going to stop any time soon, but then suddenly, without a signal, she took a sharp U-turn into a parking lot. I followed her in.

She got out of her car and ran into a nail salon. I went after her. She passed the reception desk and went straight to a lady sitting in the far back.

"Hey, Wendy, I am here. You'd better do it quick because I have a client meeting to catch. You have fifteen minutes. I just want my nails done superfast today. My client won't look at my toes, so don't worry about them. I will be back tomorrow to fix my ten little fellows down there."

Then I realized I didn't even know her name. I always saw Tom's mom from a distance. I knew she had a small business, and she always dressed nicely. Through the grapevine I had learned that she was a go-getter and she loved to work out at the gym. I went up to her and introduced myself. "Are you Tom's mom? Tom and Michael went to the same school. Mrs. Ross is their teacher. By the way, I am Vivian."

Ignoring my hand, she gave me a strange look. "I know you. You are the mother of that crazy boy who beat my son! Why are you following me?"

"Mrs. Ross said they both were at fault, and I don't believe Michael hit Tom, but that is not the reason why I am here. May I speak with you in private?"

She shrugged me off by sitting down in front of Wendy and ordering her to start the manicure. "I don't have time. If you want to talk to me, you'd better take a number."

I refused to give up, so I sat down on a chair next to her. Before I could speak, the manager of the nail salon approached me to ask if I needed a nail service. I politely declined her offer, and then I turned to Tom's mom.

As soon as I opened my mouth, she gave me a signal to stop. "You and your son must be more than satisfied now to know my husband did take a hike, but don't worry, he will not move far, and soon he will crawl back to beg me to take him back, because the lawsuit will soon run him and his little girlfriend dry.

"His little girlfriend on the side didn't know whom she is dealing with, so if your purpose here is to confirm our separation so you can cheer with your son, go ahead and make my day." She then turned to pick up Star magazine and flipped it open.

"I just want to make sure you and your unborn child are safe. You might get into a car accident soon and I want to warn you and stop that from happening."

She gave me a weird look first, and then started laughing out loud. "Are you taking prescription drugs, or is this a joke? I know. I know. You are hired by the *Candid Camera* TV program to play a trick on me. What is wrong with the Thompson family? Are you all insane?"

She turned to Wendy and asked her to finish her manicure, "You'd better wrap this up soon, so I don't need to sit here and listen to her nonsense. I am not even pregnant, to begin with."

I couldn't believe my ears. She thought I was crazy. *What if I am making a fool of myself? What if Michael was just imagining things?* I could see why people wouldn't take my words seriously. Had someone approached me with a similar claim, I would have laughed it off too.

But what if Michael's words were true? No matter how strongly I wanted to walk out that Salon door, I just couldn't bear the thought of risking two lives.

Suddenly Tom's mom turned to me again and asked, "So just for fun, when is this car accident supposed to happen?"

I didn't care about her mocking tone. As long as I could help her to stay out of the street, I would do anything.

"At 9:25 a.m." I replied, and hoped she would take my words seriously.

She turned to Wendy and said, "Now you hear it too. I am going to run into someone at 9:25. She was even accurate to the minutes. Wendy, finish my nails as soon as possible, so I can prove her wrong."

I looked down at my watch. It showed 8:59.

The Wendy lady blew some air at her nails and smiled at her work. "You are all done! Don't forget to come back to see me and have your pedicure."

Tom's mom jumped out of her seat and rushed out. Passing the front desk, she said, "put it on my account. I have to hike out of here."

My watch said 9:03. I quickly grabbed my purse and followed her out, chasing her into the parking lot. "Just a moment. Could we talk, at least?"

She waved her arms as she ran to her car, signaling me to stop following her. Then she jumped into her BMW and sped off.

I just couldn't let go the thought of her getting into an accident, so I decided to follow her. She drove crazily fast. Seeing her weaving left and right through the traffic, I was holding my breath, following as closely as possible, and at the same time trying to memorize her license plate number 2ND2NONE. Then I lost her.

As I sped up to find her, I suddenly spotted a police car that just turned the corner behind me. I hit the brake as fast as I could but it was too late. The siren blasted, the policeman signaled me to stop.

Pulling toward the right, I regretfully stopped my car and put my hands on the steering wheel. I looked down at my watch. It was 9:11.

The policeman didn't look friendly, but as he realized I was just a typical housewife, his face softened a bit. "Ma'am, do you know how fast you were driving?"

I shook my head. I had no clue.

"You were driving at least fifty-five mph in a thirty-five mph zone."

Handing my documents to him, I couldn't help but say, "Officer, I am so sorry that I sped. But I am really in a rush. Do you think we can speed up this process so I can leave as soon as possible?"

Seeing his face change color, I realized I had made the biggest mistake in my life by asking that stupid question. Right away he got suspicious.

"Why are you in such a hurry? Are you trying to catch a plane, or what? You know you could have gotten into an accident and killed someone by driving that fast?"

I peeked at my watch; 9:17. My heart started to race, so I opened my mouth again, "Officer, is there any way you can just write me a ticket? I promise I will pay it. Please let me go as soon as you can."

"Why are you so nervous? Do you have anything in your trunk?" He ordered me to open it.

I felt as if a decade had passed before he felt satisfied with his great findings. It was 9:20.

"I need to check your driver's license and insurance. Wait here."

I couldn't wait any longer. Two lives were at stake, so I begged him, "Officer, I really have to go. You see, a woman is in a great danger and I probably am the only person who can stop her from getting into a car accident. I know this sounds really crazy, but I cannot afford to take a chance because she is with child."

"I've heard all sorts of excuses, but yours ranks on top. I am sorry, ma'am. You just have to wait until we are done here."

"But I don't have time, Officer. You see, she is going to get into a severe car accident at 9:25 and it is now 9:22. Oh no, it says 9:23. We have to rush over to stop the accident. We are talking about real lives here."

The officer shook his head, "Are you an actress or are we in a movie scene right now? No one can predict such a thing? It only exists in SiFi movies. Even if what you said is true, you just have to wait." He strolled back to his car.

9:24. The digital clock on the dashboard flipped over to 9:25. I checked my watch, 9:25. I reached for the cell phone in my purse. It said 9:25.

My heart sank and my adrenaline dropped to zero. I closed my eyes and my thoughts flew out of the window. *There is no more hope. Tom's mom is going to lose her baby, and she is going to be seriously injured.* I became numb.

The officer was still taking his time processing my data. No longer did I feel the sense of urgency, so I just sat and waited. Suddenly, that same policeman ran toward me, yelling, "A car accident just took place a few streets down. I got the dispatch to survey the site. I am going to let you go this time, not because you didn't speed but because I don't have time to write you a ticket. You are lucky this time, Mrs. Thompson."

He handed me my driver's license and insurance registration, ran back to his vehicle, put on the siren and drove off. I immediately followed him. All the lights seemed to cooperate with us and stayed green until we passed.

CHAPTER 21

People were outside their vehicles conversing and pointing at the center of the intersection. A fire truck, several police cars, and the paramedics were blocking the four corners. I quickly parked my car and rushed over.

Suddenly Michael's words surfaced. "Mommy, I don't think we can stop God's clock or alter God's plan because God is the One who runs the universe. Time and space belong to Him."

What have I done? Did I make it worse? Did I push Tom's mom over the cliff? I suddenly lost it. I no longer had energy to go on.

Someone pushed me aside from behind. It was a woman who was running toward the scene. I followed her.

A silver truck with its front end terribly damaged came in to sight, and then I saw a smashed, broken, black BMW. I smelled the spilled engine oil, smoke, sweat, and blood. The driver's door was missing, and the frame of the car dented.

The black BMW was crushed, and the front license plate was missing, I ran toward the back of the car hoping to find the other license plate, and I found it dangling miserably with one screw fastened to the car.

I dropped to the ground. Somehow I felt this unknown power from above pressing me to the lowest level of the earth. The 2ND2NONE license plate was swinging in the wind from left to right as if it was mocking me.

Who is entitled to be called "Second to None"? Tom's mom? Any mortal human? Or is God trying to make a statement out of her pride?

I was told that both drivers had survived the car accident but were severely injured, especially Tom's mom. According to the eyewitnesses, Tom's mom drove through the red light and the truck hit her from the driver's side. My heart was somewhat relieved when I learned of the survival of both drivers, but *what about the baby?*

"There was no baby in the car." An eyewitness said, shaking her head. She looked at me as if I were crazy.

I immediately caught myself. No wonder countless people had thought of me as a lunatic since this morning, starting with Tom's mom, the ladies in the Nail Salon, the police, and now the street witnesses.

But am I insane? I knew one thing for certain, Michael was right. He did warn me about the inevitability of fate— or should I call it destiny, or God's plan according to Michael?

Someone tapped my shoulder. "Ma'am, you cannot stand here. You are impeding the investigation."

He sounded familiar. I quickly turned around to see the policeman whom had let me go free earlier. My mind was so occupied that I could only mutter a few words. "Sorry, I'll be out of your way."

"Wait! You are the woman who sped and got a ticket. Well, I let you go. But how did you know this accident was going to occur before it actually happened at the exact time of 9:25?"

"Officer, please just ignore my words. It is too late now. Let's just forget about it."

"So how do you know about all this? Who told you? Are you a psychic? Can you tell me my future? Should I stay put in the police department or start my own business? Wait, I might call you later about the accident. Do you know more?"

I shook my head. As I walked toward my car, I was debating whether I should find out which hospital Tom's mom had been taken to, so I could help her in some way. Then a car suddenly pulled up next to me.

"Vivian, are you lost?"

I was startled but recognized the voice. It was Pat Carey, whose son William was in the same class with Michael.

"Oh, Pat!" I was glad to see her.

"Did I startle you? Vivian, have you learned what happened to Mrs. Lovell?" She looked downcast.

Mrs. Lovell?

"Tom's mom. Remember Tom, the Little Devil in our sons' class."

"Yes. I've just learned about the car accident. It was terrible. Why are you here?"

"She was supposed to meet me at 9:30 at Starbucks this morning. I got there ten minutes early, so I was sipping my coffee until this big bang deafened my ears. I ran out and saw the aftermath of the accident, but the good news was that she survived."

"You were her appointment?"

She nodded again. "She is my investment banker. My husband and I have an account with her investment firm so we meet regularly to go over our portfolio. She told me on the phone that she had a new investment product that will generate much higher return."

Finance and investment were beyond me. "Pat, do you happen to know which hospital they took her to?"

"It is the County Hospital close by, but they might transfer her to a private hospital later." said Pat, "Are you planning to go to the hospital? Why don't we carpool? Hop in and I will drive."

CHAPTER 22

Pat and I rushed to the hospital. We confirmed that Tom's mom was indeed there. However, no matter how hard we begged the nurse, she wouldn't reveal her condition.

Suddenly an older lady stormed in, passing Pat and me, and dashed forward to the reception desk.

"I am Ginger Rider. I need to find my daughter. Some crazy driver hit her and she was rushed here. Her name is Debra Lovell. Do you know where she is? What is her condition?"

"Mrs. Rider, your daughter is in the operating room right now. As soon as the doctors come out, we will update you on her status."

Pat and I walked up to her and introduced ourselves. We told her we were there to visit her daughter as well. She looked surprised.

"I've never heard of you before. Debra only has a few acquaintances. So you both know Little Tommy, my grandson? Do you know where the bastard took Tommy and his brothers?"

We looked at each other, but neither of us had a clue. *Who is this so-called 'bastard'?*

"Can either of you tell me what happened in the car accident and who hit Debra? That bastard must have hired someone to kill Debra."

I was dumbfounded, so was Pat. *Is the bastard Tom's father, Mr. Lovell?* However, I didn't voice my question.

"So you know nothing whatsoever." She shrugged her shoulders as she looked back at us. "So you are no use to me."

"Mrs. Rider, we don't know much about the accident or your grandsons, but we are here to help your daughter in any way we can." In a way, I was trying to make up for what I couldn't have prevented. I felt guilty for not being able to prevent her daughter from getting into that car accident.

She probably wasn't used to someone's being kind to her, so she asked me, "What did you gain from this?"

"Nothing. Isn't life more important than any gain?" I didn't care how she judged me.

Gradually I saw the iceberg in her eyes began to melt. She quietly reached her hand into her purse and pulled out a pen and a notebook.

"Write down your phone number, and I will call you if she needs anything." She gave me a blank look as she handed me the note and the pen.

So Pat and I wrote down our names, cell numbers, home numbers and returned her pen and paper. Without saying a word, she turned and walked toward the narrow hall that led to the ICU.

Pat and I stood there for a while, watching her back disappeared behind the glass door. Pat finally said, "What a character! Like mother, like daughter."

Chapter 23

I never got a call from either Tom's mom or grandmother, but a few days later Pat called me, informing me that the ER doctor was able to stop Debra's internal bleeding and stabilize her condition.

"What about her baby? Were they able to save the baby?"

"You knew about the baby? No one seemed to know Debra was pregnant. I doubt she even knew. According to my doctor friend, the baby didn't survive. How did you know she was pregnant?"

I realized I wasn't supposed to know. "Pat, this is hard to explain."

"Try me."

After a brief pause, I told her about Michael's forecast about Debra's car accident and her losing the baby, and my attempt as well as my failure to stop the accident.

For a long time, I didn't hear anything from the other side of the phone, only her heavy breathing.

"Pat, are you still with me?" I asked.

"So it is true!" said Pat.

"What is true?"

"All the rumors about Michael being able to foretell the future," said Pat.

I scratched my head, not wanting to admit it. "Well, it might just be a coincidence."

Pat's voice still carried that same excitement. "Facts are facts. If Michael indeed has a fortune-telling ability, you should not be ashamed of it, but embrace it. Imagine how much he can do to help people by telling them their future or prevent mishaps. Can you imagine the prospect out there waiting for your Little Michael and you?"

I shook my head, forgetting Pat wasn't able to see my disapproval over the phone. I then realized it might not be a good idea to tell Pat this, so I kept quiet.

"Vivian, I hope you don't mind my asking— Was that you who went to the nail salon to harass Debra that morning before the accident?"

"I didn't harass her. I was trying to warn her. She wouldn't listen to me though." I could still feel that frustration.

"I am sorry. I was just repeating what my manicurist told me. They said a woman came to their nail salon that morning and harassed their client."

"Was it Wendy at the nail salon that told you the incident on that morning? Did they call me a crazy woman?"

Pat laughed. "No, Vivian, you are not crazy. They were just telling several ladies what had taken place that morning. They were not telling everyone, just a few. Anyhow, they were just...You got the picture."

I planned to hang up, but Pat said, "Wait! Vivian, that just proves what Michael said was true, and now the world knows you were right. You are vindicated. Aren't you glad?"

That was not the point. I shook my head again. I had no obligation to the world, nor had Michael.

She said, "Don't you wish Michael to succeed in life? Imagine how much potential he has! Vivian, listen to me. You now have the opportunity to convince the world that Michael is somebody special. If I were you, I would embrace it. What do you have to lose, anyway?"

"Michael doesn't want publicity, nor do I. I should have listened to Michael when he said that we should not have attempted to thwart God's plan."

"Vivian, take my advice, don't let religious stuff cripple your judgment."

"Pat, listen to me, let's put a period to our discussion today. I thought I was able to stop Tom's mom from getting into a car accident and losing the baby, but I failed. I don't want to expose Michael or Mindy to the public. We want to live a normal life. Could you please help me on that?"

"You are not Michael and you cannot speak for him. You should have his best interests in mind. What if he can save people or our country by foretelling an earthquake, a natural disaster, or even a nuclear explosion? What if he can save the world by preventing a war? You cannot hide him. He belongs to the world."

Realizing I was not able to convince Pat to see my point, I quietly hung up the phone.

CHAPTER 24

Dr. Field called several times about some possible treatments he had found for Michael's eyes. He told me of Light Filtered Contact Lenses that might help Michael from squinting in the light.

"Even though the lenses cannot correct the problem of color blindness, yet they would allow Michael to see clearly even in the glaring sunlight, and I believe further research is under way to correct color blindness."

I urged Michael to go with me to see Dr. Field but he was not enthusiastic.

"Michael, don't you want to see better? If what Dr. Field said was true about the Light Filtered Contact Lenses, you will be able to open your eyes in broad daylight."

Michael looked down at his shoes. "Mommy, I don't want to see Dr. Field."

"Why not? You don't like him? We can find another doctor if you don't like him."

He shook his head. "He is a good doctor. I didn't dislike him. It is just that...I don't want to lose you." Then he hugged me and pressed his face against my waist.

"Lose me?" I lifted up his little face, "Michael, you know you'll never lose me, but what does that have to do with Dr. Field?"

Michael thought for a moment, and finally answered, "Dr. Field likes you, Mommy. He likes you."

CHAPTER 25

After my conversation with Pat and our disagreement about Michael's future, I tried to avoid her. I was naïve. The news about Michael had already spread.

One afternoon I was on my way to pick up the groceries but was stopped by a stranger dressed in an expensive suit. He kept staring at me. At first I thought he needed my help.

"Do you need any help, Sir?" I asked him.

He gave a fake smile. "My boss and I are following a story that you might be able to help us with. A source has told us that you or your son has this special power of prophesying and we want to see if it is true."

"It is not true." I moved away from him and kept walking.

"Isn't it true that you went to visit Mrs. Debra Lovell at the nail salon to warn her about her car accident? There were at least five eyewitnesses present to substantiate the account, plus one police officer.

"Isn't it true that your son Michael told his classmate about his future before it actually happened?"

I shook my head and walked faster.

"Mrs. Thompson, if you or your son has this power, don't you think you are obligated to benefit as many people as possible? And of course, we want to be the first to help you."

I kept on walking.

"Or should we check with your son Michael first, if you refuse to answer our questions?"

He crossed the line as he suggested that alternative. I stopped and turned. Shaking my head, I tried my very best not to blow up. "What's your name, Sir? Who do you work for?"

He gave me his business card, "you can call me Joe."

I looked at his card. It said Joe Cashen and his company's name was New Phase. "Mr. Cashen, I've never heard of your company. I will call the police if you ever approach my son. He is a minor and is protected by law."

"Mrs. Thompson, my boss threatened me if I do not get your story, I will lose my job. I have a family to feed, a wife and four kids, and the economy is terrible right now."

I felt badly for him and his family. And my face must have revealed that, so he walked a step closer and asked to have an interview with Michael and me.

I didn't know what to do, but then I spotted a little smirk on his face. "Mr. Cashen, I want to help you and your family, but I have nothing to report. This is just a one-time event, nothing special. Michael said something that happened to come true. Those things do happen. Mere coincidence, nothing more."

"Mrs. Thompson, we know that this 'coincidence' happened many times. In your custody you have someone who is a savant or prophet. If Michael is a savant, you will benefit. But if he is a prophet, the world will benefit. Our world, in the midst of a bad economy and political disorder, is in dire need of a hero who can usher in hope.

"Imagine the possibilities for you and Michael. If we break the news, you will have all the media kneeling and kissing your feet. And trust me, we can angle the story any way you like it."

Joe followed me to the car. He kept talking but I closed my ears. Finally I turned to him and said, "Please leave us alone. We are not interested in your proposal."

He was still talking, with both arms waving back and forth, when I drove off. I headed toward Michael's school, because I wanted to make sure Michael was safe.

CHAPTER 26

I walked into Michael's classroom, but was told that someone had already picked him up. In a trembling voice I inquired who. The teacher told me it was Mrs. Carey.

"Pat?" I couldn't believe my ears.

The teacher looked at me in surprise. "I thought you had asked Mrs. Carey to pick up Michael. She picked up both William and Michael."

"I will call Mrs. Carey to confirm with her." I dialed her number. She picked up right away.

"Hello, Vivian?"

"Pat, the teacher told me that you had picked up Michael?"

"Yep. I have Michael here. He is playing with William right now. I didn't see you there and wanted to make sure Michael was safe so I picked up both of them. They are having so much fun."

I appreciated her concern for Michael, so I told her I would pick up Michael as soon as I could.

"No hurry. He can stay for dinner. Take your time. Michael is such a good boy, and we just love and adore him."

I thanked her again.

My heart was still not settled, so I rushed to pick up Mindy and then hurried over to Pat's house. As we drove into her parkway, Pat came out to greet me.

She gave me a hug with a big smile on her face. "Michael is having dinner with us. Do you and Mindy want to join us?"

"We really need to get back home."

"Why don't you go home with Mindy first, and I will drive Michael home after he is done with dinner."

"Pat, I already feel bad that you went out of your way to take care of Michael, and I need to pick him up."

"No problem. Let me bring Michael out." She quickly walked inside the house, and a few minutes later, she came out with Michael.

Pat gave Michael a big hug and kissed him on his cheek before she turned him over to me. Then she told Michael that he could stop by anytime or call William or her anytime. "Michael, you know we love you. Mi Casa Es Su Casa. My house is your house, and you are welcome any time."

Then she turned to me. "Did someone call you or speak with you recently about Michael's psychic ability? You know Dan has a wide network of connections…" She gave me a mysterious smile.

I bit my tongue so I wouldn't spill my disapproval. Simply nodding my head and thanking her, I rushed to the car.

"Sorry, Pat, we really have to go. Thank you."

As we drove off, I looked at the rear view mirror and saw her standing there in the driveway waving for some time.

CHAPTER 27

For the next few weeks, I received emails, calls, letters, and cards from various cities and towns and some of them didn't even exist on the map. All the letters were addressed to Michael. I opened them and found a lot of people asked Michael their future, dating prospects, or even marriage advice as if Michael were a psychic.

One letter read, "Dear Michael, you don't know me but I feel somehow connected to you. I really need your help because I am broke. I firmly believe with your vision, you know where the next big investment lies. If you don't mind revealing that to me, I promise I will give the money to the poor and the needy and end world hunger."

Another one said. "Hello, Michael. I read about you on the Internet and Tweeter, and I have been following you. I believe you are the answer to stopping an imminent perfect storm heading toward our nation. Please stand up and prophesy to our President and Congressmen about our upcoming demise, because if we don't change course domestically and worldwide, we will collide head-on into history."

Another letter read, "Dear Michael, my name is S.S Myer. I think I am the next brightest star in Hollywood, but no one has discovered me yet. Do you think you can tell people about me? They will believe you because you know the future."

"Hey Michael, I belong to this group of Prophets and we will be honored to have you speak at our camp."

So I screened calls. Unless I recognized the callers or their numbers, I just let them roll into the voicemail. Interestingly, quite a few people were pretty persistent in leaving messages, pleading to Michael to return their calls. One threatened that if Michael did not intercede to bring his girlfriend back, he would jump off the Golden Gate Bridge.

I got nervous, so for the next few days, I monitored the news to make sure no one would end his life so abruptly. Some calls were from solicitors who tried to convince Michael to come forward to make a name for himself or to save the world. They talked about "the Greater Good" with capital letters but really "the Greater Good" pointed to their own checkbooks.

Michael, to some degree, knew the attention he had drawn, but he didn't act any differently. He was still my Little Michael. We had a little chat about his fame.

"A TV station is asking you to appear on their program to help their audience solve their miseries."

Doing his homework, he didn't even look up, so I thought he hadn't heard me.

"Michael, do you want to appear on a TV show?" I asked, "I guess the world is calling you the Little Prophet now."

Mindy, sitting next to him, climbed down from her chair and ran to me. "Mommy, I want to go on a TV show. If Michael doesn't want to go, can I go for him?" Mindy asked.

I smiled as I said to her, "Mindy, they are not asking you or me but your brother. We cannot go for him. They want him to tell them their futures."

Mindy interrupted me, "I know their future."

"You do?" I was very surprised. I wondered if the prophetic genes had somehow passed down to Mindy as well.

"Just tell them they all have to die one day," said Mindy. She sounded serious.

I laughed hard. After her dad had died, we had a conversation about death and I had told her that everyone had to die sooner or later.

Michael laughed too. So I asked him again about his opinion: "I guess lots of people have expressed their interest in your counsel."

Michael shook his head, "Mommy, I only know what God reveals to me, and I know God doesn't want me to be out there in the media."

"So why did God give you this…power?" I didn't know the right word to use.

Michael shook his head again. "It is not my power, but God's power."

"What if you can help people by sharing with them God's power?"

"Mommy, people will mistaken me for God." Michael looked very serious.

"You don't want people to think you are God? You are afraid that they might worship you?"

"Because I am not God." Michael was glad that we were on the same page.

I was at a loss. I had no idea Michael was so close to God, as if he was talking about a Real Person.

"Michael, how do you know God is real? What if it is your imagination? What if this power is not from God? What if you were born with it?" I didn't have that much faith in God. If God were real, how could He allow people to suffer? If God were real, how could He steal Brian from us by cutting his life short? If God were real, how could He not have granted Michael normal eyesight?

Michael's eyes suddenly turned soft. He must have read my thoughts. He sighed. "Mommy, God is real. He is more real than any person on earth. Mommy, God is love and He loves you and me and Mindy and the whole world so, so, so much that He didn't even spare His own Son, Jesus, who came to the earth to die for us. God loves Daddy too. Death is not the end but a beginning.

"Mommy, people suffer for many reasons, but they like to blame God because it is easier that way since God won't talk back, plus it makes them feel better to blame someone else, and it gives them the excuse not to do something about the situation.

"By blaming God, people convince themselves and others that they care more than God does, but God is asking us what we are going to do about the sufferings and injustice in this world, most of the time created by us humans."

I was stunned. I had never thought about God like that before. I chewed on Michael's answer for some time. *Is this the way God sees the world also? Black or white, hot or cold, good or evil, light or darkness, right or wrong? Did God really converse with Michael or did Michael come up with this theology on his own?*

How come I cannot feel God as Michael does? Does God even love me or care about me?

Chapter 28

Then one day out of the blue I got a message from a doctor who claimed that he knew the cure to Michael's Color Blindness. He sounded very convincing. I picked up the phone and called his office.

"This is Dr. Penn. Who is this?"

"Yes, this is Vivian Thompson. I listened to your message that you have the cure for Michael's eyes, and that is the reason I am calling. By the way, how did you learn that Michael is colorblind?"

"Are you kidding? The whole world knows. People are very sympathetic about your son's colorblindness. Wait a moment."

I heard some paper shuffling, and after two minutes, he said, "Now you have my undivided attention. Yes, I believe I have a cure for your son, Michael."

I could not believe my ears. "Really? How are you going to treat him?" My heart leaped for joy.

"First off, I need to examine Michael."

"Is the cure already developed like a drug or eye surgery? Is it FDA approved? How many patients like Michael have you treated? Are they —"

"Mrs. Thompson, let's not get ahead of ourselves here. I did use the phrase 'I believe' in the beginning of our conversation. Besides, I need to ask you a few questions before we embark on our experiments."

"Experiments? So it is still in the testing phase?"

"That's not the point. I am pretty confident that I can provide the cure, so my first question is whether Michael was born with this deficiency?"

Deficiency? Is that term equivalent to disability or handicap? My mind started to race. I debated whether I should carry the conversation any further. Finally, I answered his question, "We are not one hundred percent certain if Michael was born with it. Dr. Field is working with us."

"Has Michael had head traumas when he was little?"

"As far as I remember, no." I shook my head as if he could see me.

"Besides black and white, what other colors does he see?"

"As far as I know, he sees black and white, and possibly shades of gray."

It was obvious that Dr. Penn was jotting down the notes as we went on with our interview.

"When was the first time you noticed his abnormal eyesight?"

Upon hearing the word 'abnormal', I cringed. "Not early enough. It was my fault." I hoped Dr. Penn was not thinking of Michael like one of the white mice in his lab.

"Mrs. Thompson, do you think this colorblind symptom has something to do with Michael's prophetic capability?"

"Why do you ask? I don't think they are related." I started feeling a little suspicious.

"Just checking." Dr. Penn answered. "So you don't refute the fact that Michael does own this prophetic power? And how do you prepare to pay for his medical expenses? I know a way that can help pay for it. A friend of mine has a non-profit organization that tries to raise funds for eye cancer hospitals. If Michael can be the spokesperson for this noble cause, my friend will be able to invest more funds in like kind research to benefit people like Michael."

Right then I knew it was a scam. Dr. Penn didn't have a cure. I took a deep breath, and slowly hanged up the phone.

Dr. Penn was just one of the classic con artists among hundreds. Not long after our phone conversation, I found another voice mail left by a psychologist, professor Sims, who had a low and monotone voice.

"This message is for Michael and Mrs. Thompson. My name is Dr. Sims, and I am a psychologist. Someone has brought Michael's case to my attention and after an extensive analysis, I have come to the conclusion that Michael's brain is as valuable as Albert Einstein's.

"It is my belief that Michael is not colorblind, but a genius. I believe his eyes carry the color information to his brain but his brain, by an unknown extraterrestrial intervention, refuses to process it or filter it out. So the failure is of perception, not of vision, And for his brain to do that, I believe it was intercepted by a foreign brain wave, which is probably why Michael can foresee the future and prophesy.

"However, the side effects of that extraterrestrial brain wave might cause Michael to have a personality disorder in the near future. You see, most of us with normal eyesight perceive multiple colors, and so they accept variances and tolerate differences. If someone like Michael only perceives black and white, if his world has only two colors, he is apt to develop tunnel vision or react more drastically toward right and wrong, and in many cases he won't tolerate deviations, so my conclusion is that Michael will become an extremist, either extremely good or extremely evil.

"So now his fate lies in our hands. If we steer him toward the right path by making the best use of his prophetic power to benefit society and teaching him to accept variables, he will be remembered as the greatest savant who ever lived in this millennium. Otherwise, the outcome will be forever regrettable. To make my story short, Michael, just give me a call and I will make you the second Einstein who will be forever remembered by mankind. Call me! This is all about you and your future! Don't wait!"

After I finished listening to Professor Sims' Sales pitch, I was exhausted. *How many people really care about Michael and his interest? I see none. That indeed is frightening.*

Someone touched me from the back. I turned, and it was Michael. He gave me a hug around my neck.

"Mommy, do you think we can visit Pastor Franklin? I really want to see him." Michael asked me. His eyes showed similar exhaustion.

I hesitated first. *Is Pastor Franklin going to be like the rest of the people?*

Michael shook his head. "Mommy, you don't need to worry about Pastor Franklin. He is different."

I nodded. I hugged him back. I hoped he was right.

CHAPTER 29

I didn't see the purpose of calling in advance to book an appointment with Pastor Franklin. If Pastor Franklin wanted to see us, he would.

So three of us drove about twenty-five miles to see him. Mindy and Michael were sitting in the back playing and chatting. Mindy would sing her famous songs and Michael would clap and give his sister the most generous praise.

"Mindy, you have a great voice." said Michael.

Mindy would take a curtain bow and gave her "Academy Award" platform smile. "Do you think I am better than Lady Gaga?"

I smiled. Shaking my head, I joked with her, "Mindy, you like Lady Gaga? You are too young."

"Mommy, Lady Gaga is hot right now. She has so many clothes and shoes. She has magic. She could be a princess by day and a witch by night."

Michael put his hands on Mindy. "Mindy, your voice is way better than hers."

Mindy was flattered so she asked us the next song she should sing for us, and the next, and the next, until both Michael and I got overwhelmed.

"Mindy, how about taking a short nap? When you wake up, we will be there." I said.

"But I don't want to take a nap. I want to sing for you and Michael." Mindy was not a happy camper.

Michael gave his sister a hug. "I want to hear you sing too, but you need to save some energy to sing to

Pastor Franklin, and on the way back." He patted her back like a big brother.

I smiled. Michael was always gentle and thoughtful, and on top of that he adored his sister. I wondered where their siblings' love came from — certainly not from me.

I remembered growing up, being the middle child between two older brothers and two younger sisters, I was miserable and wished I were the only child. Josh and Paul had tried their best to hide the fact that they had three younger sisters. I didn't really remember much about Victoria or Elizabeth. They played dolls and had tea parties with the dolls all the time, which was beyond me. They asked me once to join them, and told me to play a pony for the princess dolls to ride on. I refused that noble duty and never got hired again.

I smiled as the memory enveloped me. Suddenly Michael pointed at the street.

"Mommy, turn right here. The church is right at the corner."

I could tell he was excited. He stood up to make sure I turned right, but his move made me nervous.

"Michael, sit down. Fasten your seat belt."

Nodding, Michael sat back down. His eyes were sparkling and his face glowing. *Why is Michael so fond of Pastor Franklin? Is it because he is in need of a father figure?*

To my surprise, as soon as we walked into the main hall, Pastor Franklin was standing right in front of us. Looking at Michael, I could not stop myself from asking a silly question.

"Michael, how did Pastor Franklin know we are coming? Did you tell him?"

Michael smiled and shook his head. "Maybe God did."

Mindy joined in. "God must have."

Pastor Franklin at first looked surprised at our arrival. He might not have remembered me, yet he certainly recognized Michael at first sight. "Michael, what a wonderful surprise to see you."

Pastor Franklin came toward us. He shook my hand and Mindy's hand, and then stooped down to give Michael a hug.

Looking up from Michael's height, Pastor Franklin asked me, "Mrs. Thompson?"

"Pastor Franklin, you have a good memory. Do you remember every single person who has ever attended your church?" I knew it was a silly question but I just couldn't get over the fact that he remembered our names.

Pastor Franklin smiled. "I wish God had granted me that photographic memory. Truth is that I don't."

Mindy then went to hold his hand as she asked him. "So how do you remember my brother?"

Then I realized Pastor Franklin and Mindy had not met. Mindy had been with her Sunday School class when we visited his church last.

Pastor Franklin then knelt down to Mindy's level and spoke to her. With a smile, he replied, "Because your brother, Michael, is a very special young man."

"I think so too. He is a good boy!" She winked at Pastor Franklin.

"So what brings you here? Are you here to see me?" Pastor Franklin asked all three of us, but his eyes fell on Michael.

Michael nodded. "Pastor Franklin, I have some questions and I thought you would be the best person to answer them."

I said, "If you can spare us some time."

Pastor Franklin smiled and patted Michael's shoulders. "I am glad that you remember our little pact."

Michael nodded. "I remember."

"What little pact?" Mindy asked.

Pastor Franklin explained to Mindy and indirectly to me as well. "Michael and I had a little pact that he could come see me and talk to me anytime he wanted."

"Wow! Can you and I have a little pact too?"

I wanted to laugh, but held it back. "This is a man-to-man kind of talk between them, Mindy."

"Michael is a boy, not a man." Mindy's face became red. Thankfully Pastor Franklin came to my rescue. "Mindy, how about this? Let's go to my office and you can ask me as much as you want."

Mindy nodded. Pastor Franklin then led us to his office. Behind his desk was a big wooden sign, LIFE MATTERS.

"Mrs. Thompson, welcome to Life Matters church." Pastor Franklin directed us to a sitting area with three sofas, a lounge chair, and two little chairs.

"Do you sleep here?" Mindy asked.

I felt like apologizing for her but Pastor Franklin kindly replied, "Yes. Many nights I did, especially after

I spoke with God, praying for His direction or pleading for souls."

What does he mean by praying for direction and pleading for souls?

Michael nodded. "Pastor Franklin, do you sometimes feel that you are sleeping in clouds as soft and soothing as if God is holding you in His Arms?"

Pastor Franklin smiled. "Exactly! Michael! No matter how weary you are, God's embrace is amazingly tender and comforting; there is no other place you would rather be."

Michael nodded and smiled. They had a mutual understanding that Mindy and I could not relate to. At that moment I grasped why Michael had asked to see Pastor Franklin. They understood each other through their faith in God.

We all sat down.

"Michael, I am all yours," said Pastor Franklin.

Michael blinked his eyes. "Pastor Franklin, God talks to me."

Nodding, Pastor Franklin said, "Michael, you are right. God does talk to us, because we are His children."

He didn't get it.

Mindy wanted to make a comment but I stopped her.

Michael looked down for a moment, then looked up at Pastor Franklin and said, "Pastor Franklin, someone died in your family six years ago and the pain and grief has not departed from your heart. You are still in mourning. You have not had a heartfelt laugh since then, and you have been Blue…I am so sorry."

Pastor Franklin's face turned paper white. His mouth opened but no words came out. He stood up, walked toward Michael with his head low, and then sat down right in front of him. He looked directly into Michael's eyes. "I get your point. God does talk to you, directly."

Michael put his hand on Pastor Franklin's shoulder, and patted him softly. He whispered to him, "I am sorry." His eyes swelled up. He must have sensed Pastor Franklin's pain—or his own for his father's passing.

Pastor Franklin sighed. He asked, "What has God revealed to you? When was the first time you experienced it?"

"Since I can remember. I was too young to understand what God was saying, but then things would happen exactly the way God had revealed to me. I thought everyone shared the same experience, until one day God told me that He was going to take my Daddy away for a brief time. He said He was sad and my Mom and Mindy and I would be sad also."

Michael looked down at his shoes as he recalled that painful message, and then said, "I begged God not to take Daddy. I promised God that I would be a good boy and would never make my Daddy or Mommy angry." Michael turned to me, gazing into my eyes, with big drops of tears streaming down his face.

I ran to him and hugged him. Mindy joined us and started sobbing. "I want Daddy back!"

I felt a strong hand on my shoulder. At first I thought it was God's Hand touching me from above, but then I realized it was Pastor Franklin. I controlled myself. Holding Mindy in my arms, I returned to my seat.

Pastor Franklin's eyes were flooded with tears. He quickly walked away, and came back with a tissue box. He gently offered it to us.

He sat down, leaning toward Michael. "Michael, it must have been very painful for you to hear that. Trust me, I understand how you feel."

Michael nodded. He didn't reach out for the tissues. Pastor Franklin pulled one out and gently wiped Michael's face.

He reminded me of Brian in many ways. *No wonder Michael would rather talk to him than any other person on earth.*

Pastor Franklin sat back, waiting for Michael to speak.

Michael finally broke the silence, "God told me He would take Daddy's place to watch over us, my Mommy, Mindy and me. He also assured me that our separation form him would be short, and pretty soon we would be together again."

Pastor Franklin closed his eyes. "Oh Michael, you don't know how much your words mean to me. They grant me comfort. I have been enveloped by this tremendous whirlwind of grief, which turned into guilt. It has tormented me."

Michael then gave Pastor Franklin a hug. They were sharing each other's load of grief and comforting each other.

After our emotions calmed down, Pastor Franklin asked, "Michael, what else is on your mind? Do you want to share more? Anything shared in this office will not leave this room. You have my promise."

Michael looked over at me, nodded his head, and said to Pastor Franklin. "I have hurt someone's feelings by telling what was going to happen to his family…"

"Is that person your friend?" asked Pastor Franklin.

"He is in my class."

"Did you apologize to him?"

Michael shook his head.

"Why not?"

"He, along with others, laughed at me because I don't see colors. I can only see black and white. Do you think there is something wrong with me?"

Pastor Franklin smiled. "Michael, you are a boy full of surprises. God has created you with many measures of wonders and blessings, as if you were sealed by God since the moment you were conceived to be the one to fulfill His will."

I couldn't believe my ears. *No condemnation? No guilty verdict? No talk of a birth defect? Could this be possible?* His words felt like living water running through the channels of my heart. I felt a joy that I had never experienced before.

"Pastor Franklin, are you just saying that to make us feel better?"

Pastor Franklin turned to me. "Mrs. Thompson, do you believe in God?"

I was taken aback. I didn't want to say "no" in front of my kids, but I didn't want to lie to a pastor. So I chose a politically correct answer. "I've never experienced God, so I am not sure. I did attend church when I was little. However, I respect others' beliefs though." Then I changed the subject, "So were you serious when you said that about Michael that it is a blessing from God, not a curse?"

"Of course not. God never makes mistakes. He created Michael exactly the way He desired. We humans love to define normalcy, passing judgment and discriminating against others who do not share our skin color, eye color, hair color, culture, background, profession or even status.

"Michael is perfectly normal in God's eyes, so if God deems Michael normal and honorable, who are we human, to criticize His creation? It is like someone pointing a finger at Michelangelo's David, claiming the artist did a lousy job on the statue, simply because he made David too strong or too perfect.

"It might have come across people's minds that God tries to compensate for Michael's colorblindness by giving him prophetic power. I beg to differ. Michael was created in God's image, and he has God's Spirit in him. He is as normal as any person, no different from any one of us, except of course, for his extra divine blessing of giving prophesies."

"Have you met others that prophecy? Do you even think it is for real?" I asked.

Pastor Franklin walked to his bookcase, got a Bible and flipped to a certain page. "In the Book of Numbers God spoke to Moses directly. There were quite a few prophets in the Bible.

"As far as our generation goes, I have not seen one until now. But Paul the Apostle did tell us in the book of Ephesians that Christ gave some to be apostles, some to be prophets, some to be evangelists, and some to be pastors and teachers." He handed me the Bible, and helped me to turn to a book called Ephesians.

I felt sorry that I was not able to share his enthusiasm. In fact, I felt the heavy weight of the Book on my palms. *Does this Book really contain the Words of God? Is God trying to chase me down to condemn me or to love me?*

I gave it back to Pastor Franklin. "You'd better hold the Bible. Somehow it is too heavy for me."

Pastor Franklin took the Bible back. He turned to a book called Isaiah, sharing with me Isaiah's warnings of God's judgments on His people. He prophesied, at least a hundred years before they happened, the fall of Jerusalem, the fall of Babylon, God's appointment of King Cyrus to let the exiles return to Jerusalem, and above all, Jesus' first coming as God's Servant to suffer and die for the world.

Could all this be true?

Pastor Franklin didn't seem to be bothered by my doubts, but spoke with authority. "Better yet, Isaiah, in about 700 BC, told us that Jesus was coming back a second time to judge and rule as King."

I kept quiet. Michael, standing next to Pastor Franklin, started to read from the book of Isaiah.

> "The Spirit of the Sovereign Lord is on me,
> because the Lord has appointed me to preach
> the good news to the poor,
> He has sent me to bind up the brokenhearted,
> To proclaim freedom for the captives
> And release from darkness for the prisoners,
> To proclaim the year of the Lord's favor…"

Brokenhearted? Is the word "Brokenhearted" really in the Bible? Could this prophet Isaiah have peeked from his window, through more than twenty-five hundred years, right into my heart that is broken and enslaved by darkness, waiting to be freed?

I asked, "Who is this person who can bind up the brokenhearted, proclaim freedom for the captives, and release the prisoners from their darkness?"

Pastor Franklin and Michael both looked at me at the same time and answered, "Jesus Christ."

Mindy, who was sitting on my lap, responded with joy. "I know Him. I know Jesus."

That brought a smile to Pastor Franklin's face. He nodded his head at Mindy. "It is so wonderful for you to know Him at this young age. That is a blessing in itself."

His words brought back memories. Poppa and Mamma used to force us five kids to attend church when we were little.

"It is Sunday. We need to go to church." They would say.

"Why? Why do we have to go every Sunday?"

"Because I say so. Good people go to church when they are alive and go to heaven when they are dead." That was Poppa's answer.

In fact, I would just sit there in the pew daydreaming or looking around and making faces at my siblings. I don't remember any sermons, but this name "Jesus" kept popping up.

Looking at Pastor Franklin, I shook my head. "I don't think God loves me or even cares about me. He is too busy for me."

Pastor Franklin smiled as he nodded his head, "He does. He loves you more than anything, even the whole world. If He doesn't, He would not have sent His only and beloved Son, Jesus, to die for you. Mrs. Thompson, would you send Michael away to die for someone's mistake or sin?"

I couldn't believe he would even propose that question. I wanted to fight back, but as soon as I caught his eyes, I relented. He was not there to fight, but to reconcile. I found no condemnation or judgment in his eyes, or in his tones.

"Mrs. Thompson, God wants a relationship, not a religion. A Relationship's basis is love that comes from the heart and leads to freedom. A religion's basis is rules that come from flesh and lead to slavery.

"Jesus came to set you free, if you allow Him."

CHAPTER 30

Pastor Franklin explained further to Michael the roles of prophets. "All prophets bore important responsibilities for their society. All of them were appointed by God to reveal God's heart and plan to His people by warning them about God's upcoming judgments if they stubbornly chose to sin, and at the same time providing hope and comfort when God's people repented."

"So what do you think God wants me to do?" Michael then asked.

Pastor Franklin smiled and replied, "Michael, that is for you to find out. This is between you and God. Everything happened for a reason— your eyesight, your prophetic gift, and your sensitivity. Michael, God has given you many measures of gifts, and He has a great purpose in mind for your life."

Michael gave Pastor Franklin a hug. He whispered something to his ear. I saw Pastor Franklin look surprised at first, and then he closed his eyes, nodding slowly at Michael's message.

Holding Mindy, I stared at Michael. His little body somehow seemed bigger.

Leaving Life Matters Church, I was at peace. All of us were quiet as we walked out of Pastor Franklin's office. He walked with us to our car and bid us good-bye.

"You know, you can visit me or call me any time. I mean any time." Pastor Franklin gave Michael and Mindy hugs and shook my hand.

Mindy then jumped up on him and gave him a kiss on his cheek. I stood there watching, and my heart softened.

On the way back, I could tell Michael was in a very good mood. He had a glow on his face. I didn't want to intrude on his thoughts but couldn't help asking him a question. "Michael, do you think the Bible talked about those prophets' mothers?"

He looked at me through the rear view mirror. "I don't know."

"I think we should visit Pastor Franklin again, and it will be my turn. I need to find out the mother's responsibility, so I won't interfere with your important job in the world."

Mindy then waved at me in the rear view mirror.

"Yes, Mindy?"

"Mommy, Pastor Franklin would tell you it is for you to find out." Mindy imitated Pastor Franklin's voice.

She did such a great job imitating Pastor Franklin that Michael and I burst into laughter. Then I asked Michael a question that had been bothering me. "Did you share some words with Pastor Franklin before bidding goodbye?"

Michael nodded. "God wanted me to tell Pastor Franklin that He would bind up his wound in due time, and then I asked him to visit someone for me."

CHAPTER 31

That night the three of us cuddled in my bed reading *The Little Prince*.

Suddenly Michael popped a question. "Mommy, do you remember Grandpa told us a story about the rainbow?"

"What story?" I truly didn't remember. Poppa never told us stories when we were little. I wondered where he found his sources to tell Michael and Mindy stories? According to them, the stories he told were pretty fascinating.

Mindy didn't recall any story about the rainbow. "Michael, tell us the story."

Michael cleared his throat, pretending to be Grandpa. Mindy giggled. I pretended to be serious but failed, so I joined Mindy in laughing.

"Once upon a time, in a kingdom far away, there was a prince who was about to succeed to his father's throne, but he ran away from the kingdom because he felt that he was not worthy of the throne—"

"What is his name?" Mindy asked. "Does this prince have a name?"

Michael shook his head.

"Everybody has a name."

Michael gave in, "All right. Let's call him Prince Willie."

Mindy felt better that the prince had a name. She gave Michael a go-ahead.

"Prince Willie felt he was not worthy of the throne because he was a timid boy. He was in fear of everything. He was afraid of swords, horses, battles, fighting—you name it. He was even afraid of his own shadow."

"You mean he was afraid of bunnies, dogs, cats, bugs, mice, snakes, even little ants."

Michael nodded and replied, "Yes, you name it. Everything! But Prince Willie didn't tell anyone about his fear. He was afraid if someone found out about his timid nature, his father as well as the whole kingdom would be ashamed of him.

"So prince Willie told his dad the King that he needed a month to travel around the country to get familiar with the kingdom, but really his purpose was to run away so he wouldn't have to succeed to his father's kingship. He said to himself 'I could never become a great king like my father. I am not worthy of being his son or the future king to rule over the kingdom.' Of course his dad didn't know, so he blessed him and then sent him off."

"That is a sad story," Mindy said.

Michael put his finger on his lips, "Shh. Let me finish first."

"All right. All right. But it'd better be good."

Michael smiled before he continued. "So Prince Willie traveled around the world, hiding away from his own father and country. A few days before the month was over, he started missing his father, mother, and sister—"

"Oh, he has a sister? She must be a princess then. What is her name?"

184

This time I stopped her. I tickled her so she broke out laughing. I told Mindy if she interrupted the story again, I would tickle her even more. She settled down.

"Mommy, I will wrap up the story soon. So Prince Willie was sad as he walked into a remote village. He sat down next to a fountain and started to cry. It started to rain and then pour. Suddenly an old man with silver hair and a long silver beard walked up next to him, asking him why he cried so hard. Prince Willie spilled his heart out including his fear of everything under the sun.

"The old man listened and smiled. He told the prince he was an angel from God and came to help solve his problem. The prince asked the old man how he could solve his problem since he had been born with a timid nature.

"The old man then pointed at the sky. He asked the prince 'do you see the rainbow across the sky?'

"The prince nodded. 'It is the most beautiful rainbow I've ever seen.' The old man said, 'if you can walk from one end of the rainbow to the other, all your wishes will come true. The rainbow is a bridge built by God's angels to fulfill dreams.' Then the old man angel warned Prince Willie that he had to do it quickly before the rainbow disappeared.

"So the prince climbed up a tree near the rainbow, stepped on the rainbow, and walked across it. After he finished the walk, he realized he was a different person. All his fear was gone. He became a brave and strong warrior. So he jumped up on a horse and rushed home to his kingdom.

"He became the most powerful king in the whole wide world. The end."

Mindy said, "Wow! That is a great story. I like it. I like Prince Willie. I want to meet him." Her eyes closed, and she fell asleep.

I rubbed Michael's soft hair, "Michael, you do know it is a story, right?"

"Mommy, Grandpa told me the rainbow was a symbol of God's promise."

That was beyond me.

All I could do was to ask a question. "Michael, when did Grandpa tell you the story of Prince Willie and his rainbow?"

Michael answered, "It was the day after I told Grandpa about my colorblindness. Mommy, Grandpa told me I was special…He showed me that he was born with a missing rib on his left chest. He said he was special too. He also said as long as I could read newspapers, I had plenty of eyesight. He said colors exist to embellish the black and white so this world won't be too boring, but the most essential colors are black and white. Do you think Grandpa is right?"

"Yup, Grandpa is right. You are most special, but Michael, are you longing to see colors?"

"Mommy, I am. If God created colors, it must be magnificent to see them. But since I have never seen colors besides black and white, I don't really know what color is."

I didn't know how to respond to that. Just as I thought Michael had fallen asleep, he popped another question. "Mommy, do you think we can do something to help Little Tommy?"

"Why suddenly? Uh…you saw Tommy every day at school? Why do you suddenly feel the urge to help him?"

"Because Tommy has not shown up at school. God told me Tommy needed help."

I asked Michael what help he had in mind.

"Mommy, I want to start saving my lunch money in a piggy bank, and after it is full I can give it to Mrs. Ross so she can give it to Little Tommy. This way Tommy will not know it is from me."

Mindy suddenly jumped in, "I can help out too."

So we came up with the idea of "Saving Little Tommy". Michael and Mindy started putting at least half of their lunch money in a little piggy bank. I chipped in too without their knowing. After two weeks, our piggy bank was full, and Michael brought it to Mrs. Ross, offering it to help Little Tommy.

CHAPTER 32

I thought as soon as Michael handed the piggybank to Mrs. Ross, our project would be over.

Three weeks later, as I drove by the school on my way to the grocery store, I spotted at least five vans from various TV stations crowding the entrance to the school. Suddenly my cell phone rang. First it was Pat. I didn't pick up so it went to the voice mail. Then several unrecognized numbers came in. I ignored them all. Finally, when I got a chance, I listened to the messages.

Pat was almost screaming. "Vivian, you won't believe this! I just heard that all the local TV stations were all over the news of Michael's helping Little Tommy. They wanted to interview Michael, but Michael was nowhere to be found. They searched the whole school for him but still couldn't find him. You'd better come by the school."

I headed toward Michael's school. As soon as I left my car, students pointed at me and shouted, "That's Michael's Mom."

I was enveloped by TV reporters. They started videotaping me.

"Mrs. Thompson, do you know where your son is?" One reporter asked.

Another reporter squeezed his way in. "Mrs. Thompson, can you comment on Michael's ability to prophesy? Is it true that your son Michael doesn't see color?"

"I have no comment whatsoever to any of your inquiries." Then I did my best to break away from the crowd. I ran to Michael's classroom, but all the students were outside playing. Several friends of Michael spotted me and ran to me.

I asked them if they had seen Michael. They competed to answer me, but no one knew exactly where he was. One of them replied, "Mrs. Thompson, I don't know where those TV people came from, but they showed up and asked for Michael. Mrs. Ross told them to stay outside, but as soon as the class was over, Michael ran out so fast that they couldn't catch up with him. Michael ran very fast." He gave me a big smile as if he was proud of Michael's speed.

I asked his name.

"Roy. Michael is in my class. I like Michael. He is good to me. He always tried to help me when others laughed at me."

I gave him a hug. "Thank you, Roy, for telling me this. Do you happen to know where your teacher, Mrs. Ross, is?"

"We saw her walking into Mr. Klein's office."

Then the school bell rang. Class was back in session. I waited outside the classroom but Michael didn't show up. Then I saw Mrs. Ross and ran up to her as fast as I could.

"Mrs. Ross, do you happen to know where Michael is?"

She appeared worried as well. "No. I just came back from the Principal's office. Michael ran out. No one has seen him since. People are looking for him."

"What is going on? The TV reporters must have scared him off."

"Mrs. Thompson, please don't panic. We will find Michael. The TV reporters are here to interview Michael about his Saving Little Tommy's Campaign. They got word…"

"They got word of what?"

"After Michael brought his piggy bank to me and asked me to give it to Tommy, I took the liberty of announcing to the class what he had done. Other teachers found out and joined also, and, before we knew it, the principal announced to the whole school. Saving Little Tommy became a school-wide project. We were able to give a large sum of money to Little Tommy's family. Just two days ago, a newspaper reporter came to the school wanting to interview the students. He finally obliged and left, but we got even more attention from other stations today."

I noticed the students in the classroom were looking our way. "Mrs. Ross, I know you have to return to class. I will keep searching for Michael."

"I want to help you find Michael." She was sincere as she offered her help.

"Just pray—and I hope it works."

CHAPTER 33

So I ran from one end of the school to the other. I searched every corner of the campus, visited every classroom, and surveyed every restroom, regardless of gender. My heart was racing. I went back to the entrance to check on the TV crew to see if they had found Michael by any chance. When I got there, most of them had already packed up and left.

What if Michael got hit by a car because he couldn't differentiate the red light from the green? I drove up and down the streets near the school. Still no Michael in sight. Then I thought Michael might have attempted to contact me or to go home.

I followed my normal route home, and about five streets down, I spotted a little boy on the right side of the street talking with an old man. *From the back, he looks like Michael. Could it be him?* I got as close as possible to the curb, stuck my head out, and shouted before I came to a full stop.

It was Michael all right. He ran to me, followed by the older gentleman.

"Mommy, Mommy, how did you find me? Mr. G was about to take me home."

"Michael, we need to go! This is the No Parking Zone." I waved at him impatiently.

Michael opened the door to the passenger side and hopped in. Then he stuck his head out to look for the older gentleman. "Mr. G, this is my mom. Do you want to say hi to her?" He sounded really excited.

Mr. G? That name sounds weird. Where did he come from?

The older gentleman came to my side of the window, extending his hand to shake mine.

I was stunned when my eyes met his. He had the most vivid turquoise eyes that I had ever seen. They reminded me of the color of the Mediterranean Sea.

He had a full head of flawless silver hair with sideburns down to his chin. With no obvious tan, his face miraculously glowed with light. I was mesmerized. Like a robot, I shook his hand with my eyes locked on his face.

"How are you, Mrs. Thompson? Michael didn't tell me you were a race-car driver." He smiled. His voice was deep and calm, as if he had the whole world under control.

"Nice to meet you…Mr.?"

He smiled again. "Call me Mr. G. Everyone calls me that. It was a great pleasure to meet your son, Michael. Have you been looking for him? Don't worry. He is in good hands. Michael is a precious gift from God."

Michael jumped in, "Mr. G, I live a few streets from here. You can come visit me."

Mr. G nodded. "You do the same, Michael. Come by and visit me, too." Then he turned to me. "Good day, Mrs. Thompson, you are blessed."

He slowly turned and walked away.

"Who is he, Michael?"

"He lives on a ranch not far from here. Mommy, can I go visit him sometime?"

"Michael, he looked friendly, but he is still a stranger."

Michael turned to me and smiled. "Mommy, it feels like I have known Mr. G for ages. I think he is that angel in Grandpa's story."

CHAPTER 34

A TV station went ahead and reported the Michael's Saving Little Tommy story. The reporters had interviewed everyone they could find.

Mama was the first one to tell me of the reports. "Vivian, we saw the news about Michael. At first we thought it was someone else with the same name, but then the boy they described matched Michael. They showed a vague picture of Michael but it could be mistaken for some other kid. Is this for real, or a scam?"

"Mama, are you kidding? What did they say about Michael?" I couldn't believe my ears.

"Well, they reported that Michael and this Tommy were buddies. After Tommy's father was sent to jail and his mother hit by a truck and seriously injured, the family lost everything and filed bankruptcy. Little Tommy had to live with various relatives, and was treated like an orphan.

"Michael, wanting to save his little friend, initiated this piggy-bank saving plan. Then it became known to the press. The strange part is that they reported Michael had a special power to predict the future. Oh, Vivian, your Poppa wants to talk to you."

Poppa picked up where Mama had left off. "Those reporters were crazy." Poppa's voice was so loud that I had to move the phone a few inches from my ear. "Vivian, I don't get it. None of them had talked to Michael. Are they out of their minds? They concluded that Michael had a special sixth sense. They claimed that we all have it, but we don't know how to exercise it. Oh, they also called Michael Little P...What was the term they used?" Poppa was yelling for Mama's attention.

I offered the answer. "You mean Little Prophet."

"That's it! Prophet! Vivian, when your Poppa was watching the news, I thought I was seeing things. I didn't believe your Mama when she first told me they were reporting about Michael, our Michael, your Michael. They don't know Michael, and they don't know anything about our family." Poppa was not a happy camper.

"Poppa, Michael does have some prophetic capability."

"What capability?" Poppa yelled.

I tried my very best to explain to Poppa that it was not earth-shattering that Michael was born with a prophetic gift. "Poppa, I don't understand it either. Michael said God told him those things, and they happened. I guess God probably wanted Michael to become his messenger to save the world or something. Poppa, are you there? I am just joking."

Poppa was still silent. Then I heard Mama's voice, "Vivian, what did you say to your Poppa, so that his jaw dropped to the floor? He was staring at Van Gogh's 'Starry Night' that has been hung in the living room for years, as if he had never seen it before. What's going on with him?"

So I repeated what I had revealed earlier to Poppa, but made it even more brief.

"Mama, Poppa was just shocked. I don't blame him. I was shocked hearing it the first time. Michael didn't want people to know about this. It was by accident that I dug it out of him."

Mama then murmured at the phone as if she was talking to herself, "I knew that child was different from the moment he was born. He was too perfect, and too innocent, to hang around this filthy world. God must have seen that child's pure heart, and that's why He chose him."

"Hello. Mama, are you talking to me? Mama, can you let Poppa know that it is no big deal? Michael is not as powerful as some reporters have painted him. As you know, it is their job to exaggerate things. For example, unlike what they claimed, Michael didn't predict which football team would win the Super Bowl nor did he give out winning lottery numbers."

Then Mama started laughing.

"Are you laughing at my jokes, Mama?"

Still laughing, Mama said, "It is not you, it is your Dad. He said since Michael resembles him the most, he is going to the neuro doctor to have a check-up to see if he has gotten any of those special genes. Your Dad said no wonder he knew beforehand that his football team would have won the Super Bowl, because the power must have run on his side of the family."

Then she yelled at Poppa, "Michael looks nothing like you. He looks more like me, and he took those genes from my side of the family."

I burst into laughter. At that moment, I knew even though Michael's gift might sound like a big deal to the world, it did not to my family, which gave me much comfort and relief.

CHAPTER 35

"Mommy, Mr. FedEx wants you." Mindy was yelling at the front door.

"Let me see who sent it." I examined the package, but didn't recognize the name, Cameron Field.

I reached into the package, and found a letter and three tickets.

Mindy was more curious than I was. "Mommy, what are the tickets for? Did we win anything?"

The three tickets were for a Dodgers game. The letter said:

"Dear Vivian,

Since I have not heard back from you, I thought I might invite you, Michael, and his little sister to a ball game. I don't know if you are a Dodger fan, but I won't mind your cheering for the opposing team, as long as you grant me an advanced warning. Please call me. The game is this Saturday afternoon.

If you like, I can come by your house to pick you up.

Sincerely,

Cameron Field"

I was confused. Michael had once told me Dr. Field liked me, but I never took his words seriously. *Dr. Field likes me? But why?*

CHAPTER 36

The next day, I heard someone knocking on the door. Mrs. Lovell and her son Little Tommy stood there. I was speechless for a few seconds. *Does she come in peace?*

I could feel my back stiffening up in preparation for any emotional combat, but as soon as I met Mrs. Lovell's eyes, I knew I was wrong. She was on crutches and she looked thin and pale. Without heavy make-up on, she looked much older than my last memory of her in the nail salon. Little Tommy, slouching next to his mother, appeared to be short and small, and to my surprise, shy. I couldn't believe that was the same boy who had harassed children throughout his school.

I invited them in. Seeing Mrs. Lovell on crutches, I wanted to help her, but as soon as she saw my hand, she froze. Then she fought back her insecurity and allowed me to offer her a lift.

She managed to sit down on the couch, and Little Tommy, still looking down, sat quietly next to her.

I asked him if he wanted to see Michael?

He nodded first, but quickly shook his head.

Mrs. Lovell said, "Tommy, you have to. You need to do your part and I'll do mine. Remember, that's our deal?"

So I called Michael down. He didn't seem surprised to see Little Tommy, so I suggested he take Tommy to his room and play with him.

As soon as they disappeared on top of the stairs, I offered Mrs. Lovell something to drink.

"If you happen to have wine or beer, that would be fine," said Mrs. Lovell.

"Sorry, we don't drink alcohol. Anything else? Water, juice, soda?"

"I am just joking. Doctors told me not to drink alcohol anyway. I have been in and out of rehab quite a few times. Water will do."

So I fetched a bottle of water for her.

"You can call me Debra."

I nodded. "Call me Vivian."

"I know. I have known your name since the first time Tommy told me about Michael. I checked you out."

"Why go through the trouble to check me out?"

"Well, Tommy told me Michael was mean to him by giving bad reports about him or teasing him or stirring others up against him, so I believed him and tried to find dirt about you and Michael by calling around the neighborhood. I even called Pat.

"I thought Michael was a trouble maker and you were a mother who failed to discipline your own child. When you showed up at the nail salon, I thought you were out of your mind."

I wanted to explain but then she stopped me. "Let me finish or else I might not have the courage.

"The car accident really damaged my brain. I lost memory, retention, attention span—you name it. And of course you know, the baby..."

Then we both got quiet. I heard some laughter upstairs.

"Where was I? Oh, the nail salon. Right. So after you chased me out of there, I jumped into my car and raced out of the parking lot. I don't remember much afterwards, but I knew I wanted to get rid of you. Then I must have gone through a red light, at least that was what the police report and the witnesses' accounts said. They all concluded I was at fault."

"I am sorry. I should not have chased you. I should have listened to Michael, who said not to intervene. Things might not have been as bad."

She shook her head. "No. It is not your fault. In fact, I probably should have thanked you—"

"Thank me for not being able to stop the car accident?"

She smiled. "I don't know whom I should thank, you or Michael or both. You see, as they sent me through the MRI machine to examine my internal injuries, they found a brain tumor. It was malignant. So they were able to operate on me in the early stages of cancer."

She sighed.

"I was in a coma for three weeks, and when I woke up, I was a different person. No baby, no husband, no family, no money, no career, and no hair.

"My mother tried to help me, but she was already stretched too thin. I have a brother who can't take care of himself, so my mother has to do everything for him. Needless to say, she couldn't afford to have another child with insanity or a disability."

"She could have called me," I said, feeling inadequate.

Debra shook her head, "you don't know my mother. She wouldn't even ask for help from me. She has too much pride." She then pointed to her hair, "Do you like my red hair? It is a wig."

"I always like red hair. It runs in my husband's family." I smiled.

"That's right! Michael has red hair," said Debra, "I guess we do have something in common."

We both laughed. I didn't want to intrude on her privacy but I couldn't resist asking about her husband.

"He went to jail. He cleared all my bank accounts and fled with his girlfriend. The court didn't charge him on my behalf, though. It was his company who turned him in for theft and fraud. No matter what, justice was served.

"Then his creditors started going after me, so I had to file bankruptcy. I was really broke. I didn't even have the money to feed the three boys, so my siblings and my mom took turns to feed them and shelter them, until the Saving Little Tommy's Fund rolled in. For that, I have to thank you and Michael big time."

I was glad there had been a turning point for her, yet knowing the fund was limited, I offered additional help.

"That's very kind of you, but I cannot accept it. I don't want to stay crippled for the rest of my life. You know what I mean? Plus, a friend of mine from my college years has contacted me. We used to date. He saw the Michael saving Little Tommy story on TV. Through the grapevine he found Tommy and then me.

"He is now a CEO in a solid company, so he offered me a job in Arizona. After two minutes of debate, I took it. I need to move out of here and start a new life with my kids. We are moving this Friday. That's why I come by to pay my dues to thank you. Vivian, I don't hate you. I know you were trying to stop the accident and save me. No one ever did anything like that for me, not even my ex-husband, but you did. And yes, you didn't stop it, but in a way, the car accident saved me and granted me a brand new life and a new outlook. I went into the car accident a horrible person, but got out of it a better human being. Isn't that great or what?"

Before I could make any comment, she stopped me. "I am not saying I came out smelling like a rose, but just a little better, all right?"

"That's just amazing," I said.

"That means you agree with me that I was a horrible person before?" She then gave me a wink of an eye.

We laughed. After Little Tommy and Michael came down, Debra asked Tommy whether he had apologized to Michael as he had promised. Little Tommy nodded. Debra was satisfied.

As we were bidding good-bye, Michael and I walked Debra and Little Tommy to the door. I saw Debra hesitated for a moment, and then she turned to face Michael and me.

"You know who visited me at the hospital?"

I shook my head.

"Pastor Franklin."

"Pastor Franklin? You know him? How did he find out?" I was shocked and puzzled at the same time, but then I suddenly remembered Michael had whispered something in Pastor Franklin's ear.

"Pastor Franklin said a good friend of his had asked him to visit me in the hospital. He told me that God had a great plan and a future for me but it was up to me to take it or leave it. I told him God didn't care about me because He allowed all those bad things happen to me. I told him about my bad luck with my family, with my husband, with my job, with the car accident, with my lost child, and then with the newest news of my brain cancer.

"He told me that God allowed things to happen to us, good or bad, for good reasons, sometimes to draw us closer to Him. Pastor Franklin was the one who reminded me that without the car accident, my brain cancer would have not been detected. He said God loves me more than anything, but He leaves me the free will to love Him or reject Him, and as soon as I embrace Him and respond to His love, His blessing will start flowing and even showering on me because it is God's desire to grant me a purposeful, fulfilled, and abundant life."

At that brief moment, I thought I was talking to someone else, a wise and beautiful woman who spoke her feelings without fear.

Extending her hand to Michael, she said, "Michael, I know you were instrumental in helping me receive Jesus Christ to be my Lord and Savior, and I owe you my life."

Michael took her hand and shook it gently. "Mrs. Lovell, you don't owe me anything. Now as you embrace Jesus, you embrace eternal life and all the riches of His glorious inheritance."

Debra looked confused — just like me. That was too profound for us to comprehend.

However, Little Tommy had no problem getting it. He kept on nodding his head and suddenly burst out laughing. "Mom, does that mean God is going to bring all my toys back?"

CHAPTER 37

Finally everything seemed to fall into place. Michael and Mindy were doing great at school, without news reporters or doctors or psychologists on their back. I finally believed life had regained its peace. I reassured Michael and Mindy, and mainly myself that we had come a long way with bumps on the road but we had finally arrived at a safe haven.

On October Seventh, Michael turned six. Mindy and I gave him a big birthday party, inviting all his thirteen friends over. Also, as a surprise for Michael, I invited the grandparents—Poppa, Mama and Grandma Colleen who just flew in from France.

Grandpa and two grandmas gave Michael tons of toys and many books. Michael's friends ripped open the wraps and elbowed one another to claim the toys. I was amazed at how fast friendship turned sour when toys and games were involved.

Mindy said, "Stop! You should give Michael back the toys. He is the birthday boy, and he should be the one who opens the gifts. Now you boys have messed it all up."

They all stopped for a moment, and then resumed fighting for the toys.

With her hands on her waist, Mindy said, "Boys! No hope!"

Poppa went over to Mindy and tapped her head. "Mindy, you are killing all the fun. They are boys. That's the way they show their love for one another."

"Through fighting? Grandpa, were you like that when you were a boy?"

Poppa laughed out loud as he replied, " Are you kidding me? That is nothing compared to how your Grandpa used to be. *Ha-ha-ha.* We would have pulled out our guns."

I laughed. Michael didn't even care about his surroundings. He had already indulged himself in a book.

Suddenly I saw lightning flashing across the sky from left to right. I didn't know we were expecting a storm.

Colleen came up to me. "Anything you need me to do?"

She looked tired. She'd flown in red-eye. So I gave her a quick hug. "Oh, Colleen, your presence is the best gift to Michael. I cannot ask for anything more. How is your jet lag?"

She smiled radiantly, glancing through the room, and responded with a hug as well. "Oh, you don't know how much this means to me. The very last time I threw Brian a birthday party was when he turned five. Our house was also full of kids and guests. I can still smell the sweet, ticklish aroma of the beautifully adorned five-tiered cake."

I heard a thunder, loud and clear.

Colleen looked through the window and sighed. "Perfect timing for thunder! It was at that same party Nick met that woman. They shattered my world and my marriage. Nick and her husband were college roommates."

She shook her head as if she was trying to shake off her memory. "I am so sorry, Vivian. You see, the snakebite might have healed but the scar remains. In fact, today's party is going to be so great that it will wipe away and replace my old memory. It's time to celebrate!

"Thank you so much for inviting me over to be a part of Michael's birthday celebration. Jet lag doesn't mean a thing."

I was glad. Then I heard the doorbell.

Mama yelled, "I'll get it."

I had a pretty good idea who that would be, so I called Michael to help his Grandma answer the door. "Remember, today is your birthday, you are the host. You should be the one to greet your guest."

Michael ran to the door. Mama opened it. She exclaimed, "Wow! You are a big boy. I was expecting a little one."

The stranger smiled and replied, "I am sorry to disappoint you. Likewise, I was expecting a little boy by the name Michael, but it is a wonderful surprise to meet a lovely lady." He then offered his hand.

Michael yelled, "Pastor Franklin!" He jumped up on him and gave him a big bear hug. "Wow! So you are part of the surprise!"

Pastor Franklin teased him by saying, "Well, I just wanted to test you to see if God is still talking to you. I guess you didn't get the latest *Tweet* from heaven after all."

They both laughed so loud that even Poppa could hear it. I saw Mama standing there looking puzzled, so I walked over.

"Pastor Franklin, this is my Mama, and that is my Poppa, and if you look a little farther, that is Colleen." I wondered how I should address Colleen. Should I call her my "late husband's mother" or my "mother-in-law" or just "Colleen"?

Michael soon rescued me. "That is my other Grandma."

I was relieved. Mindy came over to give Pastor Franklin a hug and a kiss on the cheek. She took hold of Pastor Franklin's hand, led him into the living room, and showed him the mess the boys had made.

Poppa shook his head, whispering into Mama's ear. "Mark my words. Mindy is going to be bossy."

Mama said, "You mean she is just like me?"

I smiled. Never once had I seen Mama fighting for her own right, but when it came to her five children and now her grandchildren, she was as feisty as a hen protecting her little chicks.

I approached Pastor Franklin and offered a handshake. "So glad that you can make it!"

"Thank you for inviting me."

Michael proudly showed Pastor Franklin his treasure-- his library. A lot of books were from Brian. I couldn't figure out how Michael managed to read those serious, and dry books. Once, as Mindy flipped through a few of them, she said to Michael, "Are those books putting you to sleep? They have no pictures."

I smiled. Michael was the mini version of Brian while Mindy was the mini-me.

CHAPTER 38

"Give way! Give Way! The cake is here!" Colleen shouted.

Suddenly, all the battles came to a halt. The cake Mama had made had three tiers, with the bottom French vanilla, which was Michael's favorite flavor, the middle was strawberry, and the top chocolate. The decoration on top was a book cover made of blueberry ice cream and white chocolate cookies, titled "*The Little Prince*".

Poppa and Mama were enjoying all the commotion caused by the cake. Colleen helped me to put it down on a table. We all sang "Happy Birthday". Michael made a wish, blew out the candles, and made an announcement, "I am going to ask Pastor Franklin to say grace before we cut the cake."

Pastor Franklin came forward to stand next to Michael, and asked everyone to hold hands before he gave the blessing.

"Dear Heavenly Father, we thank you for giving us Michael. He is a blessing to us all. May You shine Your face on him and bless him abundantly. Thank you for the gorgeous cake. May whoever made it be richly blessed as well. We also pray for everyone here that he or she will embrace the greatest blessing of knowing Your beloved only Son, Jesus, who is by far the best and the perfect gift! This prayer is in Your Son Jesus' name. Amen."

"Amen."

I heard more thunders. "Is it going to rain?" I turned to Mama.

Mama looked briefly at the window, and gave me a puzzled look. "Do you have hurricanes here? The wind is blowing."

Shaking my head, I ran to the window. The sky was dark, but beams of light were breaking through. The weather report had not forecasted rain.

Several boys rushed to finish their cake, and asked Michael if they could go outside to play baseball. When Michael came to check with me, I was busy stopping Colleen from doing dishes.

"No, Colleen, you are here for Michael, and you are a special guest, I won't let you do the dishes." I tried to take the dishes from her hands.

Then I noticed Michael's presence. "Yes, Michael?"

"Could we go outside now to play? We won't go far." Said Michael.

I nodded, and Michael disappeared.

After pushing Colleen out of the kitchen, I put all the dishes in the washing machine.

As I walked out of the kitchen, I found the majority of the boys already gone but not their belongings, such as shirts, jackets, shoes, and socks.

"Where did they go?" I asked Mindy, who was playing Super Mario Galaxy.

Mindy had no idea where they had gone.

"Oh, I think they've gone outside to play baseball," Pastor Franklin said.

I turned and saw him. He was talking with Poppa. "Your father is an interesting character."

I was glad that he thought that. I gave him a smile.

"He is also very warm. He cares about you, Michael, and Mindy a great deal. He is proud of you. He said among the five children, you resembled him the most."

I laughed and replied, "Pastor Franklin, you must have heard it wrong. My Poppa would have never said that." For the next ten minutes, I tried my best to explain to him why Poppa would never have said that. Colleen came to join us. We laughed and talked, talked and laughed.

Suddenly quite a few boys ran in. "Mrs. Thompson, it is raining outside." one of them told me.

Colleen and I ran to grab towels and some shirts for them to change into.

Realizing Michael was not among them, I asked if they had seen him. One of the boys answered. "Mrs. Thompson, I saw Michael and Roy playing under a big tree earlier. They were the smart ones. I don't think they got wet."

Then I noticed the sun was out. It hadn't rained long.

Mama came out with three cups of coffee, offering them to Poppa, Colleen and Pastor Franklin. She had tea for me and herself. So five adults talked and talked. Colleen asked Pastor Franklin what he thought of 'End-Time Prophecies'.

"Since the Bible has proven itself by the fulfillment of the prophecies pertaining to history, I see no reason the prophecies pertaining to our future will not play out exactly the way God foretold. However, scholars hold different views and interpretations on this subject. Just as we all know, we have a little prophet in our midst who can share some insight…"

Then we were all shocked by a boy storming through the door. It was Roy, Michael's chum.

"Mrs. Thompson, Michael fell from a tree. He is not moving…he…" Then he screamed from the top of his lungs.

CHAPTER 39

I was numb.

Pastor Franklin rose from his seat. "Where is Michael?"

Roy ran out, so we followed him. Pastor Franklin ran first, and I was right behind him. Roy took us to a park a few blocks away. He stopped and pointed at a body lying helplessly under a tree.

Roy cried hysterically, "Michael fell from that tree. He climbed the tree, then he fell. He hit a rock."

I ran to Michael and knelt right beside him.

This can't be. This just can't be true. I am dreaming. This is a bad dream. I need to wake up from this nightmare.

Why is Michael's body cold? I screamed, "Call the ambulance! Somebody call 911!" Then my world started spinning…

CHAPTER 40

I always hate the color white, but the ER had white walls, white sheets, doctors in white, and even pale white light.

I was stopped at the doors of the operating room as they rushed Michael in. He looked tiny and defenseless lying on that long stretcher. I hated hospitals. Every memory I had of hospitals was of gnawing torture and throbbing pain.

Pastor Franklin and Colleen were next to me, but it took a while for their faces to register in my brain. Colleen rubbed my back to comfort me.

"Where are the rest of the people? Where is Mindy? Where are Poppa and Mama?" I looked around but couldn't find them.

I must have sounded crazy, because Colleen grabbed me in her arms. "Vivian, don't worry. Mindy is with your mom. Your dad and mom couldn't run with us so they stayed at home with Mindy. I just called them and they are fine. They are most concerned about Michael and you."

"Where is Michael? Why are we here?"

Pastor Franklin turned my face toward him. "Mrs. Thompson, please focus and look into my eyes. Remember, Michael fell from a tree, and we called the ambulance to rush him here. He is now in the room with the doctors. They are examining him and trying to revive him."

I started to sob uncontrollably. It was the first time I had cried since Brian's passing. I felt my whole being was shattered to pieces.

Colleen held me tight in her arms and sobbed with me.

Then I shook her violently. "What did they say about Michael? How come Michael was cold? His hands and feet were cold."

Pastor Franklin told Colleen to contact Mama to come over as soon as possible. Then he started to call people whose names I did not know. He repeated his message over and over again. "Tell everyone to kneel before the Lord and pray for Michael, his mom Vivian, and their family.'

What good does that do? To tell people to pray? What good does that do for Michael? Michael cannot hear them? His doctors cannot hear them? Besides, God is not a doctor. What can He do to help? But I was too distraught to argue.

CHAPTER 41

The door to the operating room was closed for the longest two hours I had ever endured. Then Mama showed up. That gave me a great deal of comfort. I leaned toward her and embraced her as tightly as I could. Mama held me as if I were her little girl.

Mama asked Pastor Franklin if he needed to leave. Pastor Franklin told Mama that he was at the exact place that God wanted him to be.

I turned to him. "What do you mean, God wanted you here? If God does exist and care, how could He allow Michael to fall, and now be lying helplessly in the hospital?"

Mama apologized for me.

Pastor Franklin came to sit next to me. He held my hands in his. "Mrs. Thompson, I am not God, and I cannot give you His answer. I wish I could. But I know one thing. God is true, God is alive, and He knows everything. He has His reason even when we humans don't understand. Just like a father or mother, you sometimes did things that Michael or Mindy didn't necessarily comprehend at the time, but you did it anyway because you knew the outcome would benefit them in the future.

"Can you promise me that no matter what happens, you will never let go of your hope? That's called faith."

Faith?! Faith in what? Faith in God who put me through this?

Before I could respond to his question, a person stood right in front of me. "Are you Michael Thompson's mother, Mrs. Thompson?"

I stood up right away. Facing him, I nodded with all my strength. "How is Michael? Is he awake? Can I go in now?"

The doctor gave me a brief, hollow glance. He immediately withdrew his eyes as if he were not ready to engage his emotions. Then he looked up at me with a gloomy stare, shaking his head and placing his hand on my shoulder.

"Mrs. Thompson, I am sorry. We lost him. I am so sorry to tell you the news. We were not able to revive him. It was too late."

No. He is playing tricks on me. Those doctors keep playing the same tricks on me over and over again. Don't they know it is too cruel to play those dirty tricks?

I told him to stop talking. I told him I didn't believe him, because Michael would never have left me behind. I kept shaking my head, and I told him he didn't know Michael well enough. Then I turned and ran through the door, searching for Michael's room.

I found him. He was lying on a long bed, waiting for me. I rushed to him, reached for his hand, and refused to let go. His hand was cold, so I tried to warm him up with my hands and face. Then I heard some commotion behind me, so I turned to tell those people behind me to keep quiet.

Mama was the first who ran to my side, weeping hysterically. I told her not to cry. I didn't want to wake up Michael. Mama cried even louder. Then I saw

Colleen and Pastor Franklin. They both had tears all over their faces.

Colleen took Michael's hand from me and started kissing it. I reached my hand to touch Michael's face… he was sound asleep.

Should I wake him up? I have to. We cannot stay here. We have to go home. Mindy is waiting at the house. We need to finish his birthday celebration. Michael has not opened my gift, or Mindy's gift yet. Today is his sixth year birthday and we have to go home.

Then Mama hugged me from behind, and whispered, "Vivian, my Vivian, you have to let go. Michael is gone."

What does Mama mean? Michael is gone? He is right here with me.

Suddenly I saw Michael's spiritless body. The memory returned. The doctor's voice rang through, "We lost him."

I leaped forward and covered Michael with my upper body. I started weeping and shouting. "Michael, you cannot do this to me. You promised your Daddy that you would take care of Mindy and me. You told me you would see me grow old and push me in the wheelchair. You cannot break your promise to me. You cannot be this cruel."

I saw Pastor Franklin kneeling down praying next to Michael's bed opposite to me, so I screamed at him. "Why did God do this to me? Isn't it enough to give Him my husband? Now He wants my only son too? What else does He want from me? Why doesn't He just take me? Why does He hate me so much? It would be better for Him to take me instead…Michael loves Him so much and see how God has repaid him!

"Why did you keep telling me that God had given Michael all the precious gifts because He has so much in store for him? Why did you lie to me and lie to Michael? God doesn't care. He never cares a bit how much Michael loves Him? Why? Why? Why? Pastor Franklin, say something. Why did you lie to me? Why did God lie to me?"

My voice got hoarse. I was losing my voice because I had cried and screamed so much.

Pastor Franklin stood up and walked toward me. Kneeling down again next to me, he took hold of my hand and Michael's hand, and stared into my eyes. "Vivian, God has never forsaken you, and neither will He ever. He was there with you when your husband died, and He is present right now with us. He knows exactly how you feel, because He gave His only begotten Son, Jesus, on the cross for you and for Michael. He watched His Son die.

"God is the One who gives. He is also the One who takes away. He owns us all. Vivian, you have been holding onto this grudge against God too long. You need to let go of your hate, allow God to heal you from within, and let Him grant you His peace. He created you, just as He created Michael and His love for Michael far exceeds yours.

"Michael never held His heavenly Father liable for his earthly father's passing. Can you do the same? Can you let go of your human anger toward your Heavenly

Father and allow Him to go into your heart to touch you and heal your wound?"

I shook my head as I cried, "I don't know how. I am so angry and so hopeless. I have so much hate in me. I don't know how to let it go. It is killing me. It is choking me. I couldn't even breathe."

Pastor Franklin heaved a sigh. Without letting go of my hand or Michael's hand, he lowered his head, and started to pray.

> "O my Abba Father,
> You are the Author of life. You are the Creator of this universe and our being.
> You hold the key to life and death. You uphold breath or remove it as You see fit. Nothing is impossible for You.
> You are the God who parted the sea and the river. You are the God who commands the sun and the moon. You are the God that transcends time and space.
> You are the Alpha and the Omega. You are the first and the last.
> You are compassionate and gracious, slow to anger, abounding in love, and forgiving wickedness, rebellion and sin.
> It is in Your unfailing love that I trust and it is by Your powerful name I proclaim to the world. O our God in heaven,
> You love us when we are still Your enemies;
> You redeem us when we are still sinners.
> You molded us in our mothers' womb and You counted the number of hairs on our head.

You created every cell of us, and You call us each by name.

We are Yours. Michael is Yours. You set him apart since birth.

You granted him sight, visions, and dreams.

You conversed with him in person.

O Father, our Father in heaven,

Please extend Your mercy to Vivian and give her hope.

Please show her Your true light and grant her Your great love.

Please shower her with Your salvation and prove Yourself to her.

You came to bind up the brokenhearted,

You came to proclaim freedom for the captives,

You came to release prisoners from darkness,

You promised You would never break a bruised reed, nor would you snuff out a smoldering wick.

So now we plead and intercede for Michael, for his breath, for his life. I doubt not if You breathe Your Spirit in him, he will come to life, because You are the God of life and resurrection.

May everything we do honor You and glorify Your most holy powerful name.

This prayer is in the mighty name of our Savior Jesus Christ. Amen."

He then let go our hands and prostrated himself on the floor, as if he had used up all his strength.

I was in awe of his prayer. My tears suddenly stopped flowing, and I stared at him speechlessly. I couldn't believe I had just witnessed a man who laid himself bare before God, with no reservation, pouring his heart out as if he and His God were One. As he was praying, I had experienced God's Spirit hovering upon us. I felt His Hand upon me, comforting me and supplying me His strength.

I surrendered. I realized I was powerless, helpless and hopeless. I had no control of anything whatsoever. All my past deeds rushed in, vividly and clearly. My pride, my selfishness, my unbelief, my anger, and my grudges all summed up to one word—sin. I had blamed God for everything I lacked or lost, but never thanked Him once for the things I had or the gifts He bestowed on me. I was really the heartless one.

Suddenly I was divided into three segments: flesh, soul, and spirit. My spirit, by overpowering my flesh, took control of my whole being and started communicating with God.

O God, I am so sorry. I am so sorry for all my past wrongs and grudges against You. Please forgive me. Please overlook my sins and my faults. Please give me another chance. Please help me to be a good person to the world and a good mother to my children, and please help me with my unbelief. I am the guilty one. Please don't allow Michael to pay for my wrong.

Then the tears flooded all over my face again, no longer tears of hate and anger, but the tears of reconciliation and submission. I was pleading for God's forgiveness for my pride, my anger against Him, my doubt, my denial of His existence and love, my disbelief, and all my hidden sins. God had sent Michael and many others to convince me of His love for me, but I had pushed them all away.

Then I asked Jesus Christ to be my Lord and Savior. I finally realized that I had no control whatsoever and I was ready to turn everything over to Him, including Michael and Mindy and all I had.

Then I felt this peace flowing from inside out—the peace I had never had before—the peace I couldn't even describe.

Everything turned silent. I felt no one but the One who made me. I thought everyone had left the room.

Suddenly I heard a voice next to me. "Oh my goodness. He is moving. Michael is moving…"

I raised my head above the bed, and I witnessed the miracle. Michael was moving his head and his hand.

I screamed so loud that the whole hospital heard me, but I didn't care. I just kept on screaming until the doctors and nurses rushed into our room. They were disoriented just as all of us in the room. They didn't know how to interpret the dead boy all of a sudden breathing and moving. They kept asking us "What happened? What did you do?"

Then I realized the omnipotence of the God Michael had once told me about. He indeed transcends life, time, and space. I finally got it. He is the God who cannot be mocked or put into a box. He is the God who has the final say in all matters, even in the matter of life and death. I revered Him. I was fearful of Him at that sober moment when I came to the realization of His power.

Then Michael's eyes opened. They found me. He smiled at me and I smiled back. We embraced each other for a long time.

"Welcome back, Michael!" I whispered into his ear, with overwhelming joy.

"I love you, Mommy."

CHAPTER 42

It took some time for Michael to recover completely. Mindy and I visited him at the hospital every day while his Grandpa, his two Grandmas, and Pastor Franklin visited him as often as possible. His uncles, aunts, and cousins came to wish him well, and so did his teachers and friends.

"I feel like a big shot," said Michael. He never sought attention but obviously didn't mind the love, and above all, the ice cream, cakes, balloons, candies, cookies, and lots of books and toys the visitors showered him with.

The day that Michael left the hospital there was a big celebration. His doctors and all the nurses came to bid him farewell. They hugged him, kissed him, and gave him flowers, stuffed animals, and more toys. We waved at the staff as we drove off, and we knew Michael was more than a patient to them. He was a sign of a miracle, against all medical odds, that only God in heaven could perform.

Michael told me what had transpired on that faithful day. "After the cake, we all went outside to play. Roy and I didn't join the crowd because we wanted to go for a bike ride. But then it started to rain, so we just played ball, pitching and catching the ball under the trees. We saw that the boys ran inside, but we decided to stay out because we figured the rain was going to stop soon.

"Then it started to clear up. As we were debating whether we should go for the bike ride, Roy pointed at the sky where there was a huge rainbow. He said he had never seen a rainbow that bridged the whole sky before.

"So I told Roy the story Grandpa told me about Prince Willie, whose dream was fulfilled when he climbed up and walked over the rainbow from one side to the other. I told Roy I was going to do the same, so my dream of seeing color would come true.

"Roy was very excited. He told me he wanted to walk on the rainbow too, because he dreamed of growing big and strong, and to be a football player like his brother. So we chased the rainbow. After a few blocks, we stopped at a park that had the clearest view of it. I found the tallest tree and started climbing. Roy was cheering for me. He said as soon as I came down, it would be his turn.

"So I reached the top of the tree, and I saw the rainbow right in front of me, within reach. I took my first step, and then I felt my body falling, but before I hit the ground, Jesus' big hands caught me."

"How did Jesus catch you?" I asked.

"Jesus caught me with both hands in midair but He right away lifted me to the height of the clouds, so He and I were standing side by side. He showed me all the colors He used to create the earth—the bright silver lightning, the blue sky, the glassy turquoise sea, the green grass and trees, the shining stars, the precious stones, the flowers of all seasons, the fish in the deep, the birds in the sky, the animals of all kinds—everything.

"After Jesus showed me the colors of the earth, He then painted a rainbow with His finger in the sky. Mommy, Jesus told me it was called the True Rainbow because it reflects the colors of heaven. It encompassed the most glorious colors this world has never seen: the luminous Red, the vehement Orange, the splendorous golden Yellow, the vigorous Green, the most passionate Blue, the addictively potent Indigo, and the feverishly radiant Purple.

"Mommy, the true rainbow is brilliant, gorgeous, inspiring, alarmingly real and authentic. It took my breath away. Mommy, it was beyond words and beyond my wildest imagination. Then Jesus told me all the colors were derived from 'the Light' that imparts and transmits 'the Love'. Then I realized Jesus is 'the Light' and He is also 'the Love.' He then told me to remember the colors of the True Rainbow because one day He is going to bestow them upon us when 'the New Heaven and New Earth' arrives."

I was awestruck. My jaw dropped.

"But then Jesus told me He had to send me back to Earth because He was not done with me yet, so He took me back to the hospital while you were talking to Him."

I was speechless. *Jesus saved Michael, and Jesus saved me. I owed Him two lives.*

CHAPTER 43

We missed the Dodgers game, but Dr. Field sent us an invitation to see *The Lion King*. After the show, he took us to a pizza place without knowing pizza was Michael and Mindy's favorite food. He asked us out again and again. He and I became friends.

I asked him why he went out with a widow with two little children?

"First, I was curious about you, because I always wondered what kind of woman would capture Professor Thompson's heart, for she had to be a special woman. Then I was intrigued by Michael's love for you. That means you are not only an amazing wife, but also an amazing mom.

"Never once did I desire to replace Professor Thompson in this household, because he was forever part of you, and he was Michael and Mindy's beloved father. That would never change. The only thing I aspire to do is to love and protect you and them."

Cameron, Michael and Mindy became buddies. He helped Michael to pick out the best lenses for his eyes so Michael didn't squint in the light any more.

Three years later, Cameron and I got married. All my family and Colleen were there. Pastor Franklin was our minister at the wedding. Michael was the best man, and Mindy my little maid of honor. We got married at the park under the 'The Rainbow Tree' from which Michael had fallen. Just before Cameron and I said the vows, a guest pointed at the sky and yelled, "See that huge rainbow in the sky?"

A bright smile broke out on Michael's face.

In disbelief, I looked up. Indeed, a huge, gorgeous rainbow arched across the sky. *Was it a wedding gift from God?*

I thought of Brian and his love, and the journey God had led all of us through. My heart was full of joy and gratefulness. Cameron whispered to me while the rainbow still captured everyone's attention. "I love you, Vivian."

> "For I know the plans I have for you," declares the Lord, "plans to prosper you and not to harm you, plans to give you *hope* and a future."
>
> Jeremiah 29:11